Unfated Mates
Sci-Fi Romance

GRAVITY
BETWEEN
US

ALEXANDRA NORTON

GRAVITY BETWEEN US

UNFATED MATES SCI-FI ROMANCE

ALEXANDRA NORTON

Based on a true story.

PLAYLIST

https://alexandranorton.com/gravity-playlist

ONE

ELAINA

THE SANDSTONE SURFACE of Earendel was soft under her boot when Elaina stepped off her shuttle at 3400. Her head swam as she tried to orient herself in the planet's higher gravity. Being back on solid ground after a full segment in orbit would take some getting used to.

The boxy slate-gray mechanical pack hound carried her luggage down the ramp. Elaina sighed at the underloaded machine, carrying a single backpack and a toolbelt. She strapped the belt around her waist and slung her pack over one shoulder. Flexing her toes in her boots to get a feel for familiar ground, she set off down the dusty road winding its way toward Chevron.

It was late at the edge of the universe, so the solitude of her walk wasn't surprising. But something about the quiet of the road was unsettling nonetheless. There was a tautness in the air, something Elaina couldn't quite shake—or maybe it was just her imagination, still reeling from the atmosphere pressing on her shoulders.

By the time Elaina dragged her feet up the metal staircase to her hab on the outskirts of Chevron, she could barely keep her eyes open enough to pass the retinal scan. Her backpack kicked up a puff of dust as she let it drop to the floor, soon followed by the clatter of her toolbelt. Elaina dragged herself to the bathroom, stripping her clothes as she went. She rubbed her eyes and stared at her barely visible reflection in the mirror, illuminated dimly by the motion sensor light orb at the sink. She had showered before departing the station, but now the dust of Earendel seemed to be in every nook and cranny of her body. As much as she wanted to collapse into bed, she felt her way to the shower pod instead.

Elaina lifted her face to the stream of water, letting the cascade relax her muscles. Once the grime was washed down the drain, out of her hair and nostrils, Elaina wrapped herself in a fluffy flaxweave towel and—finally—crawled into bed. That feeling from before was gone, the solitary tension of the walk. It had just been the adjustment to the atmosphere after all.

———————

"YOU'RE OFF TODAY, EL." Tuskin glanced up from the circuit board he was soldering as she entered.

"I know." Elaina trailed her hand over the metal tables lined with disassembled components. Her fingers itched to pick up the gutted satellite motherboard, to reconfigure and replace its broken parts. The urge to repair tingled at her fingertips.

"Busy down here too, huh?" she said.

"How'd you guess..." Tuskin grunted, magnified behind old specs he refused to ditch.

"Up there too. More than last shift," Elaina mused. "Something is going on up there, and here too, I think. It's... weird."

"Things break, El. It's in their nature."

She clicked her tongue. "Not like this. The wear patterns I've seen all suggest—"

"Station's old," Tuskin cut in. "Planet's old."

Elaina hummed. He was probably right. They were just going through a bad cycle. Or a good one, as far as work was concerned—more to patch, more tokens for them. Elaina should've been happy. She had done well for herself since she'd arrived on Earendel from Glacial Twelve a decade ago. There was demand for a specialist astrotechnician to do component repair planetside, and more intricate work up on the orbital station. Not to mention all the generic bits and bobs that needed patching. Elaina wasn't yet in a position to build her own hab and retire in the mountains of Alpha Prime, but she did well enough for herself.

"Go rest, El," Tuskin urged. "Take a walk. You're still recovering from orbit. Mild paranoia's routine after these longer shifts, remember?"

He was right again. Every time she returned from a stint at the orbital station, Elaina's anxiety ratcheted up for a few sols. Something about the variable air pressure, maybe.

She just needed some fresh air.

CHEVRON CITY CENTER was busy as usual, and Elaina took the quieter side streets as she navigated to her favorite teahab, a cozy little hole nestled inside an oversized cargo container. Repurposing materials was their specialty on Earendel. When you're at the edge of the known universe, on a planet named after one of the most distant stars originally detected, you take what you can get.

"She's back!"

"And awake."

Elaina cut through the tables toward the voices, pressing

a palm to the side of her neck in greeting. The corner table in the back was the coziest spot in the place, and that was where she'd always find the group—the Chevron Chatters, they called themselves. Four of them this time. She'd started attending their syncs to get out of her hab more. It was good for her to be around people, she'd realized a couple of cycles back. It was just... There were always so many other things to do! Repairs to make, new tech to deconstruct, hikes out in the arids.

Lance pushed a bowl of sandseeds toward her as Elaina took a seat. He jerked a strand of glistening golden hair from his eye. "How was it up there? A segment's a long time."

"Good." Elaina popped a seed in her mouth. The dry, crumbly outer layer gave way to a burst of sweet nectar as it cracked between her molars. "Missed these, though. The ones on station are always stale. What are we chatting about?"

"The sand. Again." Mia, the organizer of the conglomerate, sighed, adjusting her sheenlace hood around her neck.

"Not just the sand," Petra protested, smacking her palm on the table in faux outburst. Petra was the dramatic one. "The fact that it gets *everywhere*."

Petra had only been on Earendel for a season.

"You get used to it," Elaina offered. It had certainly taken her a few windy cycles to get used to the sand and dust getting... well, *literally* everywhere. Now it barely bothered her anymore. It was only the dark segments that still got to her sometimes, when the sun was dimmer and almost completely obscured by atmospheric sandstorms. It had been an adjustment after Glacial Twelve. The station in the bustling center of the Kessler Galaxy had its lighting and climate strictly controlled for optimal mood enhancement and performance.

That was fine, though. Elaina was nothing if not adaptable. Besides, her decision to move hadn't been about creature comforts. It was about adventure. The itch to go somewhere new and do something different. A fresh start in a new place to discover.

After the tea was cold, the sand topic worn out, and the sandseeds devoured, Elaina was happy but ready to trudge back home and crawl into bed with a book on her dataslate.

"It's great to have you back," Lance stepped out onto the curb next to her. "What are you looking at?"

Elaina tipped her chin up. "That."

"What? There a ship up there?"

She looked at him. "No, just the sky."

Didn't he see the silvery wisps of cloud interspersed with red and orange grains overhead, weaving through like a glistening braid stitching together two halves of the sky? Hadn't he noticed how beautiful it was?

"Oh, right." Lance grinned sheepishly. "Yeah, it is. Hey, we should sync up here sometime. You know, without the others."

Elaina's first impulse was to politely decline. She had way too many other things to do, by herself. But Lance was objectively exactly her type in seemingly every way. And... wasn't this what she wanted, in the end?

She realized he was looking at her. Waiting.

"That sounds really nice." The pressure under her ribs subsided when she forced herself to ignore it.

"Great." Lance's shoulders relaxed. "I'll ping you later and we'll arrange something."

"Sounds solid." Elaina's smile was mostly genuine. As she walked back home, her initial pang of trepidation morphed into tentative hope. Lance had been edging up to her for a while. He liked her, and maybe she could just let herself like him too.

But she had work to do, Elaina remembered as she passed by the garage. Too much work, by the looks of things. A nice problem to have. When would she even have time for Lance with all that work?

Stop it.

As Elaina climbed the stairs to her hab, that nagging disorientation of lingering gravity adjustment hit her again. She pressed her fingers to her sternum, massaging a spot there to will the sensation away.

TWO

CYAN

EARENDEL WAS hard under his boot as Cyan stepped off his shuttle at 3400. Dust puffed in a plume from the sandstone, settling quickly in the dry desert air. His first breath drew in a strange, salty tang—a sharpness that seemed to cling to his tongue. He brought up his dataslate for terrain composition, suspecting he'd find a good amount of sodium in the stone.

Only just as the damn thing began to pull up the data, the screen flickered and died.

Cyan sighed, stashing it in his jacket. Perfect timing. He ran his fingers absently through the tuft of fur on his left. Priad nudged into his leg, heavy breaths clouding in the dimness as the warg tasted the new air. Cyan scratched the beast absently, lifting his eyes to the vast expanse above them.

And then he saw it.

Where he'd expected darkness, a nebula sprawled across the night sky in vast, luminous swirls, its colors rippling like oil on water. Hazy clouds of violet and emerald wove together with threads of brilliant, shimmering blue, casting a faint glow over the landscape.

The nebula reached out from the galaxy's depths to brush against this edge-of-nowhere world, bathing the sandstone in spectral hues. Dust from his arrival caught flickers of light as it settled. The scene was surreal, vast, almost alive —and he, a mere speck in the face of all that eternity.

Cyan reached instinctively for the hilt of the sword at his hip, grounding himself as he stared upward. This wasn't just another planet—it was a world on the edge of everything, where even the sky was different, and the universe was watching.

He'd never expected to end up here. Earendel was barely reachable, and barely desirable to reach by anyone except traders, suicidal explorers, and questionable characters who had reasons not to be found. Yet the weight at his hip led him here, and so here he was. The warg on his left looked up at him expectantly, tongue lolling from his mouth.

Earendel was warm.

Cyan tried the dataslate again to no avail, then looked toward the road leading straight to an illuminated city up ahead.

Chevron, he remembered from his preparatory research. He clipped the leash to Priad's studded collar.

"All right," he sighed. "Let's go."

The dark road was empty, and heavy with a sense of inevitability. Like he was treading the path he was supposed to tread—and so he would. The sword's presence was a comforting tether. Its guidance was all he had to take. Its weight was great, but its direction always true. Cyan remained its loyal follower.

He smiled wryly to himself. Sometimes he liked to pretend he had a choice.

On the outskirts of the city, he stopped. It was a quiet street, and late enough for all the lights to be off in the windows, slatted blinds drawn shut. Beside him, Priad sniffed the air, ears pivoting. Was there danger?

Cyan turned toward a two-story block house, some kind of storefront at the bottom floor and grated stairs leading up to what was probably the shopkeeper's residence at the top. It looked new enough, with a fresh coat of green paint. The whole street looked fairly neat and well-to-do. He thought he saw the faint glow of a dataslate behind the sheer curtains on the upper floor, but couldn't be sure.

"Let's go, boy." Cyan was tired. He needed rest, and so did the warg.

IN THE CENTER, he found more life. People doing business, sitting outside bars. The outerwear on Earendel was unmistakably functional but had an odd elegance— tailored for the harsh, sandy winds yet hugging the body in ways that felt almost ceremonial. A metallic sheen woven through the rough fabrics caught the light from the nebula above. Many had layered jackets that seemed heavy and heat-resistant, their colors a blend of muted ivory, ochres, and flashes of iridescent blue—a tint he hadn't expected to find this far out from the galactic core.

Cyan found a holdover in the middle of the town square that doubled as a bar on the lower floor. At least he could get a drink on Earendel.

"We don't take pets," the keeper said gruffly, sliding a glass of brew across the bar toward him. "Not in here, and not in the rooms."

"He'll behave."

"Yeah, they all say that. That thing is huge. I don't need fur in my establishment."

"Where else can we stay?"

"Nowhere, 'less you make a friend, if you know what I mean." The keeper nodded at a group of women and two men sitting at the other end of the bar.

"I don't need those kinds of friends."

"Then you can tie *that* friend outside for the night."

Cyan worked his jaw, compelled to argue, but perhaps his first night on the planet was not the best to make enemies.

"Come, boy," he tugged on the leash, leading Priad outside.

He found a quiet spot that would be shaded by an overhang underneath the tavern windows and secured the lead there. Priad, having realized what was going on, pawed the ground. Massive claws dug trenches in the sandstone.

"I'll figure something out for tomorrow." Cyan took the warg's furry face between his hands, smoothing his brows with both thumbs. "Just lie low for tonight."

Priad emitted a whine of protest.

"Down, now," Cyan directed, pointing at the ground. He pressed on the warg's back gently until the beast circled once, twice in his spot, then flopped with a frustrated huff. "Good boy. I'll get you some meat."

HE INSISTED on the room with a window facing directly down to the spot where Priad was tethered. Inside, Cyan set his pack on the rickety chair at the wall. His broken dataslate came next, tossed on the bed like the dead weight it was. Finally, he unstrapped the sword on his back and walked to the window. Its weight was a comfort in his hands as he inspected it in the cool glow of the nighttime nebula. The dark, ashy gray of the broad tungsten alloy blade appeared to swallow more light than it reflected. It shifted under his eye, its will rippling silently beneath his gaze. The breadth of the blade spanned the length of his palm—a solid albatross that none but those it chose could have the strength to wield.

Cyan had wielded it for centuries. Or what felt like centuries anyway. Time stopped having meaning when the sword came to him, and now... well, he wasn't even sure how long it had been.

He felt ancient.

The sword was a guide and an executioner. Thrice before, Cyan had used it to end a life. The powerful schemer siphoning orbital energy in attempts to create a new wormhole. The colony ship commander who had convinced herself to murder all on board and detonate the ship in range of a population hub. The cult leader convincing followers to end their own lives en masse for "redemption." Cyan had learned a hard lesson with each—true evil, the sort his sword would guide him toward, cannot be redeemed. Cutting the rot at the root was the only way to restore order. And now he was here again, searching for whatever corruption the blade would have him uproot.

Evil does not change.

No matter that each time he used the sword, its weight had grown heavier on his back. That was his punishment to bear.

Cyan startled from his memories as the weapon of order in his hand caught the light. He stared at the blade. He was overtired and seeing things.

And yet there it was in front of him plain as day. The thin, jagged vein of hardened gold running down the length of the blade, hilt to tip... The lifeless thread he had traced countless times and knew as well as the back of his hand... It burned before him with a pulsing crimson glow.

THREE

ELAINA

HER HAND WAS steady as she clicked the wire connectors into place in the satellite solar sensor on the workbench. This tech had come from a manufacturer she wasn't familiar with, so it had taken some investigation to confirm the specs and config as best she could. If she'd gotten these wrong, the panel would short-circuit spectacularly, becoming just another piece of space junk. That wasn't what people paid her the big tokens for.

Elaina was about to test the current when the aggressive chime of a visitor walking through the sensor made her look up.

It took a moment to register the full extent of the man in the doorway. Was that *armor*? She tried not to stare at the plating on his chest and shoulders, the lines too intricate, the material too thick. It looked... ancient.

Her eyes flicked to his face only briefly, registering short black hair with a sprinkling of gray that matched the salt in his trimmed beard. A sharp jaw and mouth set tensely in a thin line. Two frown lines, subtle yet nonetheless etched between his brows, added to the relative severity of his appearance. And then Elaina couldn't avoid them anymore

—the blue-gray eyes that met hers at just that moment. She averted her gaze.

Cute. A little retrofit, sure. But cute.

It hit her then, another wave of post-orbital gravity aftershock. Elaina rubbed her sternum, trying to distract herself from the jarring sensation.

"Can I help you?" Tuskin called out.

In her peripheral vision, the man approached Tuskin's bench.

"I was told this is the place for repairs." His voice was quiet and incongruously warm in its lack of inflection, with an accent she couldn't quite place. The low, soft timbre of it was not at all what Elaina had expected from the man's rugged appearance.

"That's right," Tuskin said. "Let's take a glance."

She flexed her fingers nervously, fighting the rising sensation that *something is wrong*. She should've recovered from orbit by now. Why was this paranoia, this dread, taking so long to stabilize?

She should've taken more time off. Her tools clattered as she pushed her stool from the bench.

She felt eyes turn on her, but didn't look up. Clearing her throat, Elaina retreated to the back room. A customer shouldn't see her like this. Leaning against the wall at the chest of electronics drawers, with the voices outside hushed to the point of incomprehension, Elaina breathed deep and waited for her head to settle. If this wasn't going to resolve itself soon, she was definitely going to the doc. It had never taken her so long to get used to being planetside after an orbital shift before. Not longer than a sol. It had been three sols now and she was still not back to normal, and she did not like that.

Anchor down, Elaina.

As the feeling abated, Elaina made her way back into

the main floor, where Tuskin was back at work, alone. A new dataslate sat on a pile at the edge of the workbench.

"Said he wants it back today," Tuskin chuckled with a small shake of the head. Elaina eyed the pile of work in the queue before him—it would be a few sols at best.

"When's he leaving?" Obviously the man had been an offworlder. Wouldn't be staying around for long.

Tuskin shrugged. "Didn't ask. Said I'd ping him soon as I had news."

As Elaina picked up the slate, a familiar sensation tugged at her fingertips. A current pulling her to a thing that needed repair. "I'm ahead on that solar sat patch. I'll take a look."

"Elaina Fairan? Busying herself with a dataslate? Don't you have ships to realign?" Tuskin eyed her.

"I'm still a bit off after orbit," Elaina admitted. "Need something quick to distract myself."

"Fair enough. His connect's in there apparently. Said if we're good enough to repair it, we're good enough to find it." Tuskan scoffed. "Clearly didn't know who he was gonna be dealing with."

FOUR

CYAN

THE SANDS COLORING the upper atmosphere of Earendel were as though straight from a painting. Cyan sat on the curb next to the holdover, Priad's chin resting on his boot. The neon LED sign cast a sharp green glare on Priad's ash black fur.

They'd spent the day outside of Chevron, exploring the arid jungle areas to the north. That salty flavor to the air was stronger there than even in the city, where it was somewhat masked by the scents of life, chemicals, and food. Priad had had room to run up and down the dunes that the shrubbery areas abutted, working off pent up energy for the first time since their last trip home.

He had missed the forests and mountains he'd grown up with—if it hadn't been for the sword, he'd likely never have left his home solar system. He'd be on Gaia. Maybe with another warg to keep Priad company. Maybe with a family.

Cyan smirked wryly to himself, bringing the bottle to his lips for another sip of now-warm ale. Love had always been a fantasy. You built it—you didn't stumble around all over the galaxies in the dark hoping for lightning to strike. If he wanted it, he'd have to look. And he had no time for that; not with the weight on his back.

He frowned, steering his thoughts away from his home-world. Scratching Priad behind the ear, he smiled down as the warg met his eyes from beneath hooded furry brows.

"It will release us eventually," Cyan assured the warg.

He didn't know when, or how. But in the weeks of dreams and nightmares that followed the sword's arrival in his life, he'd gotten glimpses of a sort of *knowing* that eventually he would fulfill his task.

Or maybe he just needed to let himself believe that.

"Someday we'll make it back." Cyan gave Priad's head two firm pats. The warg yawned and flopped onto his side, tucking his paws to his chest in a gesture entirely incongruous with the fearsome beast. *This* was love. Guaranteed. Foolproof. Easy. Cyan scratched the beast's barrel chest.

The comms adhesive at the back of his ear vibrated in that moment, the bone-conducting audio announcing an unknown connection within a two-kilometer radius.

"Yes?" he answered.

"Hi. Cyan Orlogsson?"

Cyan blinked, having expected the voice of the old man he'd met earlier that day in the repair garage and instead getting something else entirely.

He could guess who it was. He had seen her.

"You're good," he smiled.

"T-thanks. It's kind of my job. Your dataslate's ready for pickup, first thing tomorrow."

"Is it fixed?"

"Well, I've got your name and connect, don't I?" the girl quipped, though he heard the hint of pride in her voice. Cyan raised a brow at Priad.

"Then I'd like to get it tonight, if I can."

"We're technically closed …"

"Please. It's important."

It's not that *important.*

Cyan turned away from Priad's unblinking stare.

The other line took a beat, thinking. "Yeah, okay. Can you get here in the next ten minutes?"

"I'll be there."

FIVE

ELAINA

IT WAS NOT TEN MINUTES. It was 2400, way past time, and Cyan Orlogsson wasn't there yet. Part of her wanted to be offended. Part of her was.

Elaina looked down at the carton of half-eaten noodles at her workbench. Honestly, she always ate dinner at the garage anyway. Not like she had anything better to do. But she could have. Who runs twenty minutes late past closing time?

The things she found in that dataslate, though... She was curious enough to be a little more forgiving.

A little.

Elaina was just about ready to give up and close shop when he arrived, still in that armored plating and the thick shoulder guards. Weren't those heavy?

"Sorry I'm late," the man said with a look that didn't seem that sorry at all.

"It's sand off the helix."

No, it's not.

Only the agitation that had been building melted away as soon as he offered her a broad, open grin, and something about it struck her as so innocent... so... boyish? How could anyone possibly be mad at that smile?

Or maybe she was just too curious about what she'd found in that dataslate. There was something off-axis about this guy, though not in a bad way. Or maybe in a bad way. Elaina wanted to find out.

He was already taking a seat on the stool across from her workbench as if this were anything other than a quick handover.

"Cyan Orlogsson," he said, clasping a large hand to the side of his neck.

"Elaina Fairan." She returned the greeting. "Here's your dataslate. All patched. I had to crack the passcode."

"Ah, so you found my list of victims?"

A laugh escaped her, so sudden that she had to cover her mouth, and the way something sparked in his eye and his brows went up a bit for a moment made her look away.

"If I did, I wouldn't tell you, would I?"

"Smart."

"How did you break it?"

"Hmm?" He cocked his head.

"Your dataslate. How did you break it?" She slid the slate over to him.

"I... didn't, actually." Cyan Orlogsson scratched his chin through his beard. "Or I don't know. It must've gotten damaged in the landing somehow, when I got here. Or maybe I just sat on it and didn't notice." He chuckled.

Elaina frowned. "I don't think that's it..."

"Tell me."

Something came to attention in him. His expression didn't change, but the air around him stilled somehow. He was curious, and... well, she'd been dying to tell this to someone who was actually curious for a while. But also, for some reason, she didn't want to come off like a crazy person to this man.

"Just something I noticed during the repair. Similar patterns of damage to other devices that have been failing around here, and in orbit."

"You work in orbit?" He perked up.

"Yeah, up on the orbital station. One-segment shifts."

"Segment?"

"Umm..." He was *definitely* not from around here. "A segment is thirty planet sols."

"Ah. A month."

"Month." A clue to his origin, perhaps?

"Anyway," Elaina shook her head, "it's probably nothing."

Cyan propped his elbows on the workbench and leaned forward. His eyes, deep silver in the low light, fixed on her in a way she didn't like, but didn't... not like either. "What if it's something?"

Good question. What if it *was* something?

"What brought you to Earendel?" she changed the subject. "And what is that thing about?"

She had been dying to ask about the sword on his back, its hilt jutting up over his left shoulder. And other things too.

He paused, as if weighing how much he wanted to share. "It's part of my work."

"What do you do, joust?"

His laughter was full and deep, straight white teeth flashing handsomely.

Crap.

"You know jousting?"

"I read."

Yes, she knew what quadrant he was from now. But

where in the quadrant? One of the inner edge stations surely.

"Not quite. I'm tasked with keeping the order of things."

"Like a Quadrant Cloister agent?" Elaina raised a brow.

"Something like that." He paused, his expression growing distant.

"So the things in that dataslate…"

"You snooped."

"I patched."

Cyan raised an eyebrow, obviously knowing full well it was a bunch of crap. She hadn't needed to go through those docs for repair. But he'd told them to look through the slate to grab his comm info. How was anybody supposed to *not* follow that trail?

"I come from Gaia," he said.

"Fuck, I'm sorry…" she blurted out. "I mean…"

"It's all right." Cyan smiled. "At least now I know you guys swear the same on Earendel."

What did you say to someone who just lost a century in the outside world to journey through a wormhole? Had he lost anyone? Had there been anyone to lose?

The smile faded from his lips. He must've known what she was thinking.

Elaina looked at him, *really* looked at him. The graying stubble, the worn hands, the sword. He wasn't just some stranger with an outdated outfit. He was a relic of humanity's origin world.

"How old are you?" she asked.

Cyan frowned, then looked off at the wall behind her. His fingers twitched slightly, one by one. Was he… *counting?*

"I don't know. Time is strange now. I guess it always was. I have lived about forty Gaian years, I think."

"Give or take a century? Fuck. Sorry."

Elaina wanted to kick herself for the tasteless joke, but Cyan barked out an explosive laugh that made her want to make him do that again.

"Something like that," he said through a chuckle.

"So what made you come here?" she prodded. Was that too much? Was she prying? She wasn't great with personal questions. Answering them, sure. Asking, not so much.

"Duty," he answered flatly, the hilt of his sword reflecting the overhead halogen lights as he shifted in his seat.

Elaina nodded, getting the hint. "Well, I hope you find what you're looking for here. Come back if the dataslate starts fritzing again."

"I kinda hope it will," he said quietly, and she tried to both decipher the meaning and suppress the warmth on her cheeks at the same time.

OUTSIDE, the first thing that hit her was the giant warg tied to a halopost. Its silver eyes were glowing mirrors of Cyan's own.

"That's Priad," Cyan introduced as Elaina kneeled next to the beast. The warg rose and shook itself out from head to toe, tongue lolling out as it smiled up at its master, then turned its intense gaze to Elaina.

"Same color eyes," she grinned between them. She held out the back of her hand, offering it for sniffing. "Hey, Priad." The beast gave its permission and she reached up to stroke the coarse fur at the side of its neck. "Boy?"

"Yes."

She marked the pride in Cyan's voice behind her as she

admired the warg. There weren't many of those on Earendel. Not many animals in general. She missed that.

"Is he all the way from Gaia too?" she looked up at Cyan.

"He is."

"Well traveled, aren't you!" Elaina addressed the beast, trying to keep it light. "Well, I'm going that way. Enjoy your stay and good luck with the order-keeping and all." She rose, smacking the dust off her knees with her palms.

Part of her wished that he'd do the knightly Gaian thing she'd heard about and offer to walk her to her hab.

Don't be stupid. You don't want a stranger to know where you live.

She wouldn't invite him in or anything. She just wanted to talk more. A little more. Maybe a lot more.

SIX

CYAN

THE WAY she got down to pet Priad without hesitation sparked an impulse in him.

"Lunch tomorrow?" he asked suddenly, the words out before he could think them through.

The girl looked up, surprised. The corner of her mouth quirked in a smile he sensed she was trying to keep to herself.

"Sure," she said. "I'd like that."

AS CYAN LAY in bed that night, tapping through Earendel's terrain analyses on his dataslate, he thought back to what Elaina had said, about the patterns of damage in devices on Earendel and in its orbit. There was more there to learn. It might just be the first clue he needed to figure out why exactly the sword led him to this edge of the universe.

But perhaps he was just looking for reasons. He'd been growing lonely even before he left his home galaxy. Not often alone, but lonely nonetheless.

Cyan had managed to avoid thinking about the family he'd left behind what to him felt like a blink ago. He was in a brand new quadrant, a brand new world. There was too much to think about, making it easy to not focus on the fact that a Gaian century had passed while he was in that wormhole, following the sword's calling. Everyone was dead.

Cyan wrenched his mind off the topic.

Elaina Fairan was undeniably beautiful, though somewhat odd... a little in her head. A little jumpy maybe.

He could work with that. And he had work to do. This might just be the lead he needed. Or maybe he just wanted to see the girl with that smile and those eyes again.

EVERY LEAD so far had been a dead end. Other than grumbling about unreliable, decrepit tech or frayed chip readers, nobody had much of anything to say. The sword wouldn't have led him all the way here unless it was *big*. So where was it? Where was the source of corruption on Earendel?

The planet was oddly hospitable, more than he'd expect considering its lack of proximity to literally anything and the reputation of its residents, earned seemingly purely for being hermits or pirates. He should have known the stories would be greatly exaggerated. They always were.

"Who runs this place?" Cyan asked the old woman behind the counter. She had been Gaian as well apparently —gone through the wormhole nearly seventy years ago with her entire family.

"The city?"

"The city, the planet."

"The city *is* the planet. There're some tribal outposts

beyond the arids, but nobody pays them much mind and they keep to themselves."

Those must be the real hermits.

"Chevron is run by a council," the woman exclaimed. "Supposedly elected, but more like whoever steps up gets the spot."

"Sounds like a great recipe for a power struggle," Cyan mused.

The beads in the woman's hair clacked together as she shrugged. "Not really. Most of us don't care much for politics, long as the hinges keep oiled. Like this stupid token reader," she grumbled, slamming the heel of one bony hand into the device on the counter in front of her.

"Right." Cyan glanced at the embedded local time display in his holovision.

Damn. He was late again.

"Who are the council members right now?"

"Only one I know is Tuskin." The woman shrugged again. "There are five or six more, or something like that. Tuskin's—"

"I know of him." Cyan wrapped up the conversation with a warm smile. "Thank you."

———

CYAN SPOTTED Elaina from the end of the street, sitting on a bench outside of the diner. He slowed his step, allowing himself more time to take her in.

A far cry from the cargo pants she had on in the garage the night before, this time she wore a knee-length layered ivory wrap skirt made from a fabric that shimmered with iridescent threads, catching the light as she shifted in her seat. The material draped asymmetrically, with intricate folds that gathered on one side. A close-fitting white tunic plunged deep from her collar to her sternum, exposing a slim line of skin between small breasts.

She had one leg crossed over the other, a sandaled foot making small circles in the air as she scrolled through her dataslate. Vine-like straps wound up the curve of her calf from her heel, ending just below her knee.

He enjoyed the style on Earendel, he'd decided. And she looked good in white.

Cyan had to strain not to stumble forward as Priad jerked on his leash, impatient with his master's suddenly slowed pace.

"Elaina."

She looked up when he was standing before her.

She smells good.

"Sorry I'm late," Cyan said, tying Priad to the end of the metal bench. "I got caught up."

"Thank you," she said diplomatically.

Oh yeah. She's annoyed. None of that helix sand stuff this time.

Punctuality had always been a problem for him, but it was made worse with the arrival of the sword. Minutes, months, years passed in a blur he couldn't quite grasp. Cyan had found certain strategies, when needed. But keeping up with the world—or maybe the world keeping up with him—had always been a challenge.

They sat side by side in the cookhouse, some sort of local bird eggs and noodles sizzling on their wireless hotplates.

Elaina's hotplate promptly fizzled out.

"Of course," she said wryly. She grinned at him sideways, making a sweeping motion with her hand toward the dead gadget. "Exhibit A."

"Of things breaking around you?"

"Well, not around *me*, just this planet. Wait..." She sat up straight and stared at him, deadpan. "Maybe it is me!"

He laughed. "Elaina Fairan, the destroyer of hotplates."

They ate slowly, drawing out each bite as the conversation veered from Elaina's work, to where she came from, to what brought her to Earendel of all places.

"I wanted somewhere new, but stable. And where I could do interesting work, with good nature and good air."

"Will you stay?"

She shrugged. "I don't really get attached to places."

"What about to people?"

She paused there, staring at a spot on the counter between them. When she answered, she picked her words slowly, deliberately. "I think I want to get attached to people. To someone. I want to let that happen."

"But you don't?"

She glanced at him briefly, then tucked a strand of dark hair behind her ear. The dangling white earring in her lobe flashed in the overhead light. "That's a little scary, don't you think?"

"It can be," Cyan agreed. "But I think it's worth it. I want that too."

He sensed the hesitation there as she gnawed her lip.

"I've had a couple of long relationships," Elaina finally said. "But there's just so much of the universe to discover, and... how do you know when you've found the right person to do all that with?"

"I think you're meant to feel it."

"I've always just felt like I've had a foot out the shuttle. But I don't think I want to do that anymore." There was a determination in her voice that made Cyan wonder if she wasn't still trying to convince herself of that. "Not with the right person."

"When did you decide this?"

"A couple of cycles ago. I've been trying. I think I'm getting better." She looked at him with a sincerity that took him aback. "I think it's possible for that to exist."

"What?"

"...Love, I guess?"

"Me too," Cyan said quietly.

As they finished lunch, Cyan found himself wanting more time. It felt easy, sitting there, talking about things with someone who felt oddly familiar even though they came from opposite sides of the universe. But the more familiar weight settled heavier on his back. His hand flexed instinctively toward the sword's hilt, its presence reminding him who he was. What he was supposed to do.

"I'll ping you tomorrow," Cyan said once they were outside in the midday sun. Days were *long* on Earendel. Double Gaia's twenty-four-hour cycle.

"I'd like that," Elaina said, loitering on the curb.

But as Cyan walked away, trepidation gnawed at him. How much time could he really afford this? The sword's fated duty was more than just a burden. After all these years, it may as well have been a limb. Without it, who would he be? Just another man, searching for meaning in the stars.

SEVEN

ELAINA

ELAINA SAT across from Lance at the teahab, smiling at the appropriate moments, nodding when he talked about his latest project. It was fine. He was fine. But the whole evening felt like she was watching herself from a distance, like someone else had taken over and was going through the motions of what a good date should be.

It was orbits apart from her lunch with Cyan the sol before. She wasn't sure what had happened there, but she knew one thing—whatever chemistry she'd felt with him, it wasn't here. The connection wasn't the same.

But maybe that was all right. Lance was objectively hot, and kind, and *local*. Elaina hadn't even asked Cyan how long he was planning on staying on Earendel.

Maybe part of it was that it seemed premature for such a pointed question. Besides, with the right person, location was just another logistic.

"You're blushing."

"I'm sorry, what?" Elaina looked up from her teacup.

"You're blushing," Lance flashed a white grin. "I'm really enjoying this too."

"Oh. Right." She hid behind a sip of tea. "Same."

After lunch with Cyan, Elaina really felt like cancelling on Lance and just going for an evening hike alone out in the arids.

But she was making an *effort*, and dating was meant to be fun, and meeting people was good.

And before she randomly stumbled into a fierce-looking offworlder with a weirdly compatible sense of humor and interests, Elaina had thought Lance had potential. It would be stupid to put all her sandseeds in one palm.

Luckily, Lance didn't suggest they do this again when they got up to leave. He would, though. She could tell. And under normal circumstances, she would say yes. She should *still* say yes. But at least she didn't have to try to work up her enthusiasm on the spot.

But as she walked back to the garage to wrap up some work for the night after the date, what Elaina really kept doing was checking her comms.

EIGHT

CYAN

CHEVRON'S "COUNCIL CHAMBER" was a modest space sharing premises with a distributor of solderglue, whose warehouse was on the lower floor.

Cyan sat in a small office, his attention drawn to the window behind the councilwoman across from him, where plumes of sandstone dust swirled patterns in the orange-tinted sky.

"Your world is beautiful," Cyan said.

"I know." Mari Saban finally looked up from the holographic projections hovering atop her desk. She leaned forward in her seat, stippling bony fingers on the table before her, and looked at him expectantly. "How can I aid you?"

"I am a newcomer to your planet, and—" Cyan began.

"I know you are," the councilwoman interrupted. "And I have questions about that, though usually we try not to ask many around here." She paused. "Stand by a tick."

This quadrant's terminology was taking Cyan some time to get used to, but he got the idea. Mari Saban's attention drifted back to her projection, quickly tapping the control pad on her desk. Her eyes flicked to him briefly before returning to the data streams. "This dock situation's been a scrapheap for sols."

Cyan tried to follow the data on the projection, but it was hard to decipher the rapid stream of Universal.

"Oh." The councilwoman sat up and pressed a finger to the back of her ear. "Bless the winds."

She pushed herself up from the desk and proceeded to pace, clipped steps tapping on the concrete floor. Her beige wraparound shawl flowed heavily behind her, the straw-like material it was woven from whispering as she moved. Its seamless hood draped heavy and thick around her neck, reminding Cyan of a fat brown python wrapped around its mistress's shoulders.

"Yes, I've seen the latest update," Mari snapped. "No, I don't care how long it's been down. We need to be able to charge tolls before the next fleet lands."

Cyan pretended to gaze out the window. Perhaps this visit would be more valuable than he had thought. Whatever the source of universal chaos was, it was not the councilwoman. Tuskin, however, the old man from the repair shop, kept coming up. Could he be involved?

This was irregular. It had been rare to be drawn to a universal imbalance in which the root cause was not obvious. There was a time, once—early—that Cyan had made a mistake. It had happened on the Martian colony, when he thought the perpetrator threatening Mars's orbit was the colony chieftain himself. It was not until Cyan completed the execution that he realized it was the chieftain's wife who was pulling the strings to siphon orbital energy for the creation of another wormhole.

His sword had struck down the wrong man that day, its weight doubling overnight. A price Cyan would continue to pay. But he had corrected the situation swiftly. The sword always found its mark, in the end.

The councilwoman sighed. "Fine. Tonight is fine. Fleet arrives in three." Mari gave a sharp nod to the wall. "Good. She's the only one I trust with this at this point. Those toll machines are ancient."

Her tone lightened with palpable relief. "At least we'll have someone competent on it soon. The contract mechs are... well, they are what they are."

Mari Saban turned back to Cyan, rubbing her temples, and he quickly cleared the small smile from his expression. "Apologies. Planetary dock's been chaos. Toll machines are the latest casualty. So." Her brown eyes settled heavily on him. "Cyan Orlogsson. Let's talk about you."

Cyan rose. "Thank you for your time. I'll let you get back to your reports."

———

THE SUN DIPPED low over the arid plains, casting long shadows across the sand. The day's winds had died down, leaving only a gentle breeze in their wake. He and Elaina walked side by side, their footsteps crunching in rhythm in the sandy grass. Priad padded ahead, nose twitching as he explored the foreign terrain. He was a dark blob against the pale ground as he wandered into the distance against the setting sun.

"Do you ever get tired of all this sand?" Cyan asked, watching a thin plume dislodge from Elaina's hair in a breeze.

She glanced over at him with a little smirk. "You mean the endless desert wasteland? No, can't say I do."

Her laughter rang out into the empty space around them when he gave her a playful shove. Her dialect was blunt, the edges of words cut sharply, the consonants weighted like stones. It gave her voice a kind of rawness, unrefined but genuine, and he found himself liking it.

"It's not that bad," she said. "At least we've got some view. Could be stuck on one of the interior worlds, where the only thing you can see are the stratus towers."

"Stratus towers?"

"Really tall buildings. Like… thousands of levels tall."

"Skyscrapers," Cyan concluded.

"Sure. Those, I guess."

"I've seen enough of both—deserts and concrete." Cyan sighed, his gaze drifting out over the endless horizon. "I prefer the forests."

"What are those like on Gaia?"

Cyan's mind drifted back home, softening. "They're dense. Wild. Alive. The trees grow so tall they blot out the sun, and there's this deep green everywhere you look. The air is cool, and there's always water somewhere close since the Rejuvenation—rivers, streams, even just the dew on the leaves." He paused. "I grew up with the mountains just beyond the woods. Used to climb them as a boy, try to see how far I could get. The world felt endless back then."

"The world *is* endless," Elaina smiled, leaning in conspiratorially. And she was right. He supposed it was. "It sounds beautiful."

Cyan nodded, brushing the hilt at his hip, a reminder of why he'd left that beauty behind. The sword had brought him to Earendel for a reason, and until he fulfilled his duty he couldn't go back. But then, after…

"Would you ever move?" Cyan asked. Of course, "move" was a loaded term. People moved within a quadrant all the time. That was easy. Having to jump to the other end of the universe through a wormhole as everyone you love ages and dies in real time is another kind of move entirely. Not one he would ever ask of her.

She threw him a sly sideways grin. "Depends on the company."

Would she ever actually consider it, going that far? She seemed so free, but freedom could be flighty. Would she be doing it for him, or for her own curious whims?

They walked a few more paces before Elaina gave him a sideways glance. "Do people on Gaia ever read palms?"

Cyan blinked, caught off-guard. "Why do you ask?"

She shrugged. "Some guy back at the port was from that quadrant. Said he'd had his fate read in his palm. I figured maybe it's the same back where you're from."

Cyan chuckled. "It's an old Gaian tradition. You read the lines on someone's hand to predict their future. Readers would tell you the shape of your life just by looking at your palm."

Elaina raised her brows, a playful glint in her eye. "You believe in all that?"

"No." He met her gaze, his heart picking up just a bit. "But it's a good excuse to take someone's hand."

Without thinking much about it, Cyan reached out, wrapping his fingers around hers gently. Her breath hitched subtly as he lifted her hand and turned it so he could see the faint lines etched in her palm.

"Here," he said quietly, running his thumb along one of the lines, tracing it from her thumb toward her wrist. "This is your life line."

Elaina's long dark eyelashes brushed her cheeks as she looked down at her hand in his. She bit her lip, hiding a small smile.

"And what does it tell you?" When she looked up at him, that close, he found himself needing a moment to stumble for the words.

Cyan leaned in a little, pretending to study her palm intently. "It tells me... you're stubborn."

Her laughter cut through the desert air. "You didn't need to read my palm for that."

"No." He smirked, letting her hand go with a soft squeeze. "But now I have proof."

They kept walking, the air between them now filled with an unspoken understanding, and Cyan found himself wanting to hold onto it.

"Anyway," Elaina said, breaking the silence, "I don't put much stock in that fate stuff. My life's never been so neatly mapped out."

"How so?"

She shrugged, but her tone was a little too casual. "My mom was big on superstition. Used to study neutrino oscillation patterns for some hint of the future. Didn't seem to make her any happier, though."

"Where do they live?" Cyan asked.

"My mom's on Senta Station, and Dad is… I'm not sure. We're not close. They were always off working, so I was mostly raised in the hive."

"The hive?" Cyan tried to recall, but he hadn't seen that term in his research.

"It's like… community caretaking. Kind of a niche thing in this quadrant," Elaina explained enthusiastically. "You end up with a lot of parents instead of just two!"

"And that never bothered you?"

"Not really." She kicked a rock in their path, sending it skittering ahead. "You get used to it. They were busy, and I was fine. I didn't really think about it."

Her words were light, but maybe a bit too practiced. But before Cyan could respond, a faint howl rose up from the direction Priad had wandered.

Elaina stopped, scanning the horizon. "Is he okay?"

Another call—sharper, more urgent.

"Stay here where it's safe," Cyan told her, unsheathing his sword. "I'll be right back."

NINE

ELAINA

"STAY HERE" wasn't really in Elaina's vocabulary.

Her blackweed boots crunched against the sand and foliage as she ran after him. Cyan was fast, his silhouette already disappearing into the rolling dunes ahead.

There was another howl. Closer now. *Priad*.

Elaina broke into a full sprint, determined to keep up. Maybe it was the stubbornness Cyan had joked about earlier.

She ducked beneath the low-hanging branches of some scrubby shrubs, breaking out into a small grove where she finally saw them—Cyan, standing still, and Priad, drenched and triumphant, with a long, sinewy creature dangling from his mouth. The warg's eyes gleamed with pride.

Elaina stumbled to a stop, catching her breath. The limp river snake's iridescent scales glinted in the fading light. Priad's tail slashed back and forth as he looked from her to his master and back again, showing off his work.

Cyan turned, raising an eyebrow. "I told you to stay."

Elaina shrugged, still panting. "Looks like he caught his dinner."

Priad gave a low, proud growl, dropping the river snake at Cyan's feet with a soft thud.

Cyan exclaimed something guttural and melodic that must've been Gaian as he bent to ruffle Priad's proud cheeks and neck, praising the work.

"Is it edible?" He glanced back at Elaina.

"Oh yeah. River snakes are a delicacy. He's got good taste."

Cyan grinned, kneeling to inspect the snake under the warg's watchful eye. "How do we cook it?"

Elaina sighed. "Well, I'm a vegetarian, but I'll make it for you. You've got to eat a river snake right."

A flicker of amusement crossed his face. "I'll gather some firewood." He stood and made for the undergrowth. Priad stayed firmly in place next to his kill.

Once Cyan's broad silhouette blended into the fading light, Elaina turned her attention to the tall sandseed stalks near the stream bank. She brushed her fingers through their fluffy purple heads. Their sweet musk hung in the air as she tugged a few free, gathering enough burnt orange seeds for a small meal.

On his return, Cyan worked with purpose, arranging the sticks and dry grass methodically before pulling a flamer out of his pocket. The fire lit fast, and he added more straw until it burned steadily.

From another pocket, Cyan extracted a small knife. He took the snake from Priad's watchful shadow and splayed it out on a rock.

"I take it we need to gut it?" he asked, glancing at Elaina.

She nodded, relieved that he volunteered to do this part of the job. "Most of the organs are a delicacy, and they get baked in the body. But you need to remove the head and everything from the third intestine down. Just make a cut about there." She indicated the spot.

Cyan got to work, following her instructions precisely, each movement deliberate as he extracted the third intestine, bowel, and reproductive organs.

"Thanks," Elaina said, coming to kneel beside him. "I'll do the rest."

"You sure?"

"Sure. I can *touch* meat, you know, just not put it in my mouth," she grinned.

He flipped the knife in his hand, holding it out to her hilt-first. Elaina took over, cutting the meat into portions and skewering it with a sturdy branch. Normally she'd do this with an electric slicer back at the hab—the primitive prep was kind of exciting.

"Give him a piece," Cyan said, nodding toward the warg. "But tell him to 'sit' first." He paused. "But he only speaks Gaian."

"All right," Elaina said. "What's 'sit' in Gaian?"

"*Sitka*."

"*Sitka*?"

"Try it."

She turned to the warg, who watched the raw meat in her hand with pure lust. "*Sitka*," she said, trying to sound firm under the endearing influence of the beast's hungry gaze.

The warg's butt plopped onto the ground, sending up a plume of dust. His tail thumped excitedly.

"Good boy!" Elaina exclaimed, then looked up at Cyan. "How do you say *good boy*?"

"*Dobro boyak*," Cyan said.

"*Dobrro bojyak*," she tried as she gave the meat to Priad, who promptly swallowed it whole.

The rest she roasted, standing next to the fire while Cyan reclined against a boulder a few steps away.

He hadn't been in his full armor that night. Instead, he wore loose-fitting trousers made of a fabric that seemed both sturdy and lightweight, with subtle metallic threading that shimmered under the firelight. His long-sleeved tunic was fitted at the shoulders but relaxed through the torso, with intricate black stitching along the cuffs and neckline. The muted earth tones of his clothes spoke of practicality, yet there was a touch of a certain craftsmanship that made them different from anything she'd seen on Earendel. Despite their understated appearance, the clothes had an almost ceremonial air that reminded her of how different their worlds really were. He was from the cradle of humanity itself, and she was from the most developed industrial quadrant in the known universe. There was so much she could learn.

Elaina arranged the sandseeds on a flat rock and set it on a small pile of charred coals that still glowed red for light roasting. Then, settling on the ground next to Cyan, she held out a piece of roasted meat. "Here."

He looked at it, then at her, a mischievous glint in his eye. "Feed me?" he said, the corner of his mouth quirking up.

The request took her aback. Good thing it was too dark for him to see her blush. Elaina cleared her throat, but leaned closer and held the piece of meat to his lips. He took it from her fingers, watching her, and she wondered what he was thinking.

Cyan chewed slowly, the teasing look in his eyes softening.

"Thank you," he said, his voice low.

Elaina nodded, her fingers still tingling from the brief

contact, and turned back to the fire, enjoying the heat brushing her face.

"So..." she started, offering the next piece to him a little more confidently once he swallowed the first. "Do you make a habit of eating things your warg drags out of streams, or is this a special occasion?"

Cyan laughed boldly. "Let's just say I've had worse. This is goddamn delicious."

"Thank you!" Elaina was delighted to hear a genuine Gaian 'god' reference. She'd have to ask him more about that. "You helped."

"Team effort."

They let the crackling fire fill the space between them, enjoying the silence of the falling night, and the nebula brightening overhead.

"Have you done this before?" she asked after a while, gesturing to the fire, the setting, the simple, primitive feel of it all.

Cyan nodded slowly. "Many times. My sister and I used to do this, actually. Sit by a fire like this in the forest back on Gaia."

Elaina smiled softly, picturing it. "It sounds peaceful."

"It was." The quiet longing in his voice tugged at something deep inside her.

Elaina hesitated, watching the firelight flicker across his face. "How did your family react? When you told them you were leaving."

Cyan's sighed, staring into the flames. "They were sad, but they didn't question it much. Just not their way, I guess."

Something inside her ached at the quiet resignation in his voice. She wanted to say something comforting, but she'd never been very good at that, and the words were elusive.

"Here," she said, taking a fresh skewer of river snake and a handful of roasted sandseeds. "Have more."

Cyan looked at her hand, then up at her, a whisper of understanding passing between them. His fingers were warm as he took the offering, and the silence between them was enough.

TEN

CYAN

BACK IN THE holdover that night, Cyan placed the sword onto the sill. Earendel's nighttime nebula cast a silver pool along the blade's edge. The golden vein pulsed with the remnants of a faint crimson glow that faded but never quite disappeared since the first night he arrived on the planet.

He turned to the desk and pulled out the old Gaian tome he'd brought as a keepsake. The weathered cover showed a boy with a sword, sitting on a majestic white steed —a glimpse of an age long past. He brushed fingers along the ridges of the illustration before flipping the book open.

Battles and quests filled the brittle pages—knights on horseback, mythical creatures, ancient kings. Cyan flipped through the book, each illustration a reminder of stories he had grown up hearing by childhood fires.

He paused on a chapter depicting a Gaian fortune teller —an old woman with deep-set eyes and a knowing smile, surrounded by faded runes. Elaina had asked him about palm reading before... He wondered if Earendel had its own stories, its own truths hidden in its legends. Perhaps there were clues there, waiting for him to discover. Chevron was a

45

modern city, flooded with scrappy tech and buzzing neon. But the tribal lands would be a different story.

As Cyan reached for his dataslate, his promise to Elaina, delivered before they parted, came to mind. He said he'd chime her about meeting again. At the time he'd meant it. But now, there was a discomfort to the expectation. And he needed to work. He *would* chime her. Just later.

Instead, he activated the slate and pulled up a map of Earendel's outskirts. The tribal lands spread beyond the city's boundary, reaching past the dunes into the untamed wilds.

He traced potential routes with his finger. Those lands called to him, something about them feeling right—a place untouched by the technological grip that now failed the rest of the planet. He had thought the disturbances on Earendel —the malfunctions—were part of why he was here, but what if the true source of corruption was out there, in the plains? He needed a bigger picture.

The walk with Elaina had felt too easy, like slipping into a rhythm that wasn't his own. He couldn't afford to let it distract him from what needed to be done. The connection between them had gone beyond simple attraction. There was something more there—and it could easily pull him off course.

Cyan leaned back in his chair, eyes falling back to the blade. He stood and crossed to the window, staring out at the quiet streets below. The flickering lamps along the roads brought back memories of the fire he and Elaina had shared —the warmth of it, the dry air, the way she had handed him sandseeds with that tentative compassion and fed him snake meat with nervous, gentle fingers. Cyan shook his head, pulling himself back to the present.

He grabbed his pack from the corner, tossing in a few essentials. Tomorrow, he'd leave for the tribal lands and find whatever waited for him there. The sword had drawn him here for a reason—something beyond the bond forming with Elaina.

But what if she were part of the reason too? She'd noticed the technical anomalies before anyone else, and had been working on putting things back together. She was restoring the order of things too, in her own way. Like him.

He silenced the thought, sliding the sword into its sheath. There would be time for that later.

Maybe.

ELEVEN

ELAINA

CYAN'S PROMISED chime hadn't come that night, nor the sol after that or the one after. Elaina chastised herself for being as disappointed as she was. She barely knew the man. Usually she wasn't the constant comms type, but if you *tell* someone you're going to chime them, isn't it just common decency to do it?

It was just the conversation. That was what she enjoyed so much. Not the sharp eyes or the smile that looked so pure as to be almost childlike, or the hands that weren't really her type at all.

Lance's hands were objectively finer. Long fingers on broad palms. A little less stubby.

Elaina rolled her eyes at herself in bed, setting her dataslate aside. Cyan was here for work. It had only been a couple of sols. People forget.

But they don't forget me.

Maybe he just didn't feel the same things she had. Maybe he clicked with everyone like that, and their time together was nothing special. Besides, he was surely still processing the loss of his past. Elaina was being selfish— *something* brought him here at the cost of his life back on

Gaia, so it had to be important. He had bigger things to worry about than keeping a promise to a stranger.

It didn't matter. People were flakes sometimes. Maybe she'd just latched on too quickly after a lifetime of holding back. Cyan was just a passerby anyway. No point getting excited.

She grabbed her dataslate again and read the message that Lance had sent her two sols ago.

> I had a lot of fun the other night. Want to
> do it again this spanend?

Yes, she dictated the reply subvocally through the bone-conducting mic and earpiece behind her ear.

But she hesitated, fingers hovering over the screen. She *should* say yes. She should keep her options open. Cyan had been a nothing but a brief moment in a life that had always been full of people coming and going. But part of her didn't want to hit send. Part of her wanted to wait just a little longer, to see if this thing she felt had any chance of being real—or if it was just another fleeting moment, like all the ones before.

Elaina sent the ping.

I had a lot of fun too, she added for good measure.

ELAINA HAD RESOLVED to busy herself with work and social activities over the next few sols, only that didn't happen.

"I need you to go back up," Tuskin told her when she showed up at garage two sols later.

She paused with her coffee halfway to her lips.

"So soon?"

"Yeah."

"It's… I just recovered, Tusk." She sighed. That disorienting feeling of imbalanced gravity had only just begun to subside, as had her fixation on the tech issues she'd noticed. But then, he knew this wasn't to protocol and yet he was asking anyway. Her curiosity got the better of her. "What's up?"

Tuskin gave her a defeated look. "Things are really haywire up there. Got the comms this morning. They need someone stat. Someone good."

Pride welled within her at the implication. It took her many cycles to feel like she was actually good at her job, though others had always recognized it. Validation was always nice. Besides… now she was curious. Elaina's hunch that something was off here was getting more real by the sol, and maybe now it'd finally be vindicated. And she'd be the one to solve it.

"I can go now."

Tuskin *tsk*ed his tongue, eyeing her through those fishbowl glasses like he knew exactly what she was thinking.

"Shuttle don't leave for another sol. Go pack, I'll have a sled here for you at thirty hundred tomorrow."

TWELVE

CYAN

THE WIND SWEPT across the dusty plains, carrying with it the dry, earthen scent of Earendel's tribal lands. Cyan stood on a small rise, gazing out at the sandstone flats stretching endlessly into the horizon. Low-set settlements dotted the landscape, blending into the taupe earth as if they had grown naturally from it. Sundried reeds marked the borders of the largest village, their rustling whispering stories only the winds could understand.

He'd spent all day in those settlements, trying to translate the local Universal dialect as best he could, his dataslate his only lifeline to understanding. The children had laughed at his efforts. They had been playing with sticks nearby, weaving through the rows of reeds, until the sight of a stranger and a giant warg caught their attention. His accent had amused them, and he couldn't blame them. At their age he would have laughed too.

The plains were nothing like the lush forests and snow-capped mountains of Gaia, but their unvarnished rawness resonated with him all the same. There was something so simple about it. He wondered if Elaina had ever been out here, to see the tribes and their quiet resilience. The thought slipped away as quickly as it had come, and he shifted his stance, watching the dry grasses sway in the wind.

The trip, if he were being honest, had been fruitless. The language barrier hadn't helped, but even beyond that, there was no grand corruption or underlying disorder to uncover. Earendel, in its own way, was more devoid of conflict than many other places he'd been. The separation between the advanced, utilitarian city of Chevron and the remote tribes seemed natural, unforced. There was more than enough land to go around, and the sparse population meant territorial disputes were rare—aside from the occasional skirmish over water. Despite its arid nature, Earendel had a surprising abundance of small streams snaking through its plains. It wasn't a bad place to settle down, all things considered.

But it wasn't Gaia.

Cyan turned back toward Chevron, convinced anew that that was where his mission lay. He absently scratched Priad's massive skull. The warg leaned into the touch, watchful eyes scanning the horizon. Cyan's other hand found its way to the hilt of his sword, resting on the anchor. The familiar weight—the cold steel, the promise of purpose—felt thin these days. He'd come here on a mission, driven by the pull of fate, but somewhere along the way, he'd let himself get... distracted.

By someone who, through her repair work, was just as much a part of trying to piece together the fractures of Earendel as he was.

Someone who'd been waiting on him.

The last time he'd seen Elaina, he saw in her eyes something that unsettled him—a hope that flickered in and out of his mind, forcing him to confront things he'd rather keep buried. It held a silent invitation for him to stay close. Instead, he'd thrown himself into his work. And then—

He'd forgotten her.

Forgotten to ping her, to follow through on something so simple it bordered on laughable. The guilt twisted his stomach as he entered Chevron's crowded streets, the noise of the city barely registering.

I'll reach out tomorrow, he told himself. Maybe that would ease the tension building in his chest.

She hadn't contacted him either. Hadn't chastised him or asked where he was. Elaina was busy with her own duties, just like he was. She probably wasn't even bothered.

Yes, she had her own life here, and could never fit into his. After his mission, Cyan would leave. Probably go back home to Gaia until the sword called on him again, though there wouldn't be anyone left for him there by now. Nevertheless, *that* was his place. Why complicate both their lives when the logistics of their futures were worlds apart?

THIRTEEN

CYAN

THE HOLDOVER he'd been staying at was a relic, an aged testament to the fringes of civilization. The kind of place where chrome had rusted, and the neon signs outside buzzed faintly, struggling against the decay of time. The paneling barely held together under layers of synthetic varnish. The windows, shielded by faded metal grates, were clouded from years of exposure to the sandstone grains and fumes of the city. Old ale, machine oil, and recycled air seemed embedded in the walls.

Cyan liked it that way. It was a reminder that even in this corner of the universe, some things refused to change.

The keeper hadn't given him shit about Priad anymore, once it became clear Cyan wasn't going anywhere much and could pay. He moved toward the bar, intending to find a quiet corner, when a familiar figure hunched over a large battered freeze box lying on its side caught his eye.

"Tuskin," Cyan called, and the mechanic straightened to face him.

The old man wiped his sweaty brow with the back of his hand, then patted the freeze box with a solid thump.

"Give me a hand, will ya? Gazz wanted this antique thing patched, and now it's my job to get the damn thing upright."

Cyan grabbed the other side of the bulky appliance. Together, they hefted it across the floor and pushed it upright.

"I'm surprised you could even fix it," Cyan muttered, his muscles tensing with the effort. Tuskin let out a gruff laugh.

"Surprised myself. Thing's older than the sandstone, and with everything else on its last leg around here... But—" He gestured to the back with a thumb. "Gazz's got a soft spot for antiques. Can't say no to nostalgia."

Once they'd set the box down, Cyan turned toward Tuskin. "I hear you've got a lot on your plate around here."

The old man grunted. "Could say that. Maybe my Elaina was right. You know El, the—"

"I know her," Cyan said, an uncomfortable doubt creeping in. Tuskin's need to clarify who Elaina was meant he hadn't come up in their conversations. Had he been on her mind at all?

"Well, she's figured somethin' was wrong for a while. I ain't convinced. Then again, they are pulling her up to orbit for an emergency shift..."

Cyan blinked. "What?"

Tuskin shrugged, his gaze shrewd. "They got it real bad up there. Ox leaks and all. It ain't good for anyone to be up there so frequently, but can't be helped."

"When is she leaving?" Cyan asked, trying to keep the excitement from his voice.

Tuskin raised an eyebrow. "Why don't you go ask her? She's up on the rooftop."

"Here?"

"Yup." Tuskin watched him shrewdly and Cyan didn't like that look.

But he nodded, already stepping back toward the stairway up. "Thank you."

THE ROOFTOP BAR WAS DESERTED. Figured, since the "bar" part looked like it hadn't been opened in decades. Rusted and plastered over with solar wrap, there wasn't much up here other than old steel benches.

Cyan spotted her immediately, bent over something at the corner table, dark hair falling forward as she worked.

She didn't look up at his approach, though he knew she must've heard him. A small device lay in pieces before her, tools arranged with precise purpose across the table's surface.

"Can I join you?"

Her hands stilled for just a moment before resuming their work. "Sure."

Cyan sat, watching her fingers move with practiced efficiency over the scattered components. "What are you working on?"

"Atmospheric density scanner." Her tone was clipped, professional. "The bar owner's using it to predict sandstorms."

"And it's broken?"

"Nope. Just making it better." A slight smile tugged at her mouth. "The base model only gives basic pressure readings, but with a few tweaks..." She held up what looked like a miniature processor board. "Now it'll track particle density too. More advance warning."

"Tell me more."

Elaina's eyes lit up as she explained the modification, most of it going over his head but worth hearing her excitement. Cyan found himself leaning closer as she grew more animated, gesturing with a tiny screwdriver.

"Sorry," she caught herself, finally meeting his eyes. "I get carried away sometimes."

"I love that." He meant it.

She studied him for a moment, then pushed the device toward him slightly. "Want to see how it works?"

"Show me."

Elaina's smile widened as she walked him through the scanner's inner workings. Her initial aloofness melted away as she lost herself in the explanation. Cyan watched her hands move over the machinery, sure and confident. He'd felt those same hands on his skin just a few sols ago, feeding him. The memory sent heat crawling up his neck.

"You're not listening anymore, are you?" she asked quietly.

"I got... distracted." He cleared his throat, forcing his gaze back to the device.

She sat back, crossing her arms. The playful moment faded. "You know, I know we barely know each other, but when someone tells me they'll chime me and then doesn't, it gets confusing."

"I'm sorry. I got caught up with my work."

"I get it. You've got your mysterious mission, your sword, your... whatever this is. But I waited."

Her directness caught him off-guard. He hesitated as she started plucking tools into the toolbelt at her side.

"You're right," he said. "I'm not... good at this."

"At what? Keeping promises nobody asked you to make?"

"At wanting to make them."

Her expression softened. "You don't owe me anything, you know, I just—"

"I know." He watched as she finished gathering her things.

Elaina stood, slinging her bag over her shoulder. "I'm heading up to the orbital station soon. Lots of things breaking up there lately." She gave him a measured look. "In case you were wondering where I'd be."

She was giving him another chance, he realized.

"Be careful up there," he said quietly.

Her smile was small but genuine. "Always am."

Cyan sat long after she'd gone, watching the nebula come alive over Chevron. The sword at his back felt heavier than usual, its presence a reminder of everything he couldn't have.

It was only then that the obvious idea hit him—one he should've thought of already. He'd gotten no leads down here, yet he knew the sword didn't take him to this place for nothing. Whatever he was meant to find, whatever purpose had brought him to Earendel, it wasn't on the surface. It had to be up there, waiting for him in orbit.

It was time to move. He'd worn out his options down here, and every instinct he had told him that his next step lay up there, on that orbital station. Elaina might be part of it, or maybe she wasn't, but he was going to be there regardless.

As he returned to his room, Cyan's thoughts zeroed in on what had to be done. Whatever was waiting for him up there, he was ready to face it.

FOURTEEN

ELAINA

THE NEXT EVENING she was buzzing. Her fingers itched to get themselves on more evidence, and more work. This might be the perfect opportunity for her to not just prove herself again, but also investigate exactly what was going on. She'd found common patterns in the damage down on planetside equipment, but the tech on the station was much more intricate, and designed for more advanced diagnostics. They had debuggers she didn't have access to down here. Maybe she'd dig in and figure this thing out once and for all. Finally connect the dots of her hunch.

She counted down the hours as she threw some clothes, dental powder, and other necessities in her pack. She was mentally going through the first diagnostics she'd run on the core systems up on the station on her way out the door, so in her head that by the time she collided face first with a metal barricade it was too late to stop it.

"Ouch!" Elaina stumbled back, then immediately went for the electric prod on her toolbelt before following the line of armor up to find none other than Cyan Orlogsson reaching out to grab her shoulders and keep her stumbling form upright.

"I'm so sorry," he blurted. "I didn't mean to startle you."

"It's... okay." Elaina caught her breath, releasing her hold on the prod. His eyes followed her hand. Elaina frowned. "What are you doing here? And... how'd you know where I live?"

"Your boss told me," he explained. "I swear I'm not stalking you. Too much."

There he was again. She'd tried to stay annoyed at him the sol before, after he waltzed up to her at the rooftop and started flirting like nothing happened after leaving her hanging for sols. It had been annoyingly disarming. "You're at my hab, Cyan."

"Right. But I swear Priad and I have a good reason."

A huff from behind Cyan's legs made Elaina crane her neck to look past him. It was already dark, and all she could spot of the warg in the shadows were a pair of glowing silver eyes.

"Hi, Priad." She received panting in response. Elaina turned back to Cyan, still looming in her doorway. "So what's the reason? Is your dataslate broken again? I kind of have to—"

"Go to orbit, I know. I'm here because I need to come with you."

Huh?

"What do you mean?"

"Look," Cyan told her. "Something is going on here. But I think you know that. Finding out what is part of my work."

"Right. The mysterious 'keeping the order of things.'"

"Exactly. I need to come with you. And I can help."

"Oh? You're also an astrotechnician?" She was being bratty, but something in her *knew* he could help. And another thing was irrationally excited about having a travel mate. Maybe *this* travel mate.

"Nothing that impressive." Cyan chuckled. "But I'm

good at feeling these things out. I know it's too early to say 'trust me,' but..."

Elaina picked at a seam in the strap of the pack she had slung over one shoulder. She supposed if he were asking her to come along, he couldn't get up on the station on his own. Maybe he wasn't authorized. But with her... people trusted her up there. Letting a complete stranger tag along would be a stupid, impulsive move that would surely be driven by something other than professionalism.

Fuck it—she had decided to take more chances on people. And for better or worse, she wanted to take one on this person specifically. Maybe it was time to finally follow her intuition instead of overthinking everything in her life all the time.

"All right. Just don't blow anything up, okay?"

Cyan recoiled, placing a palm on his plated chest with faux indignation. "I'm not a *terrorist*, Elaina."

"Better not be." She brushed past him and into the cool night air, a small smirk on her face. "Let's go."

FIFTEEN

CYAN

THE SHUTTLE to the station technically took three hours, but the time disappeared and Cyan did not believe it was the distortion of the sword this time. He and Elaina were the only passengers on the shuttle, strapped into seats across from each other. The pilot had tried to put Priad in the cargo hold, which Cyan aggressively refused. He strapped the warg into the seat next to him. Or rather, the three seats. Priad was not a small warg.

"This is related to the hunch you had?" Cyan asked once they were through the ear-splitting roar of the launch and outside the atmosphere. "About the devices?"

Elaina looked up and to the side, hazel eyes rimmed by dark rings catching the light from the holos overhead. She knew the answer—she was just considering whether she wanted to tell him.

"It might be," she said finally. When she looked back at him, he wasn't prepared, and he turned away from her rapt attention. "But now I get to find out. And you get to do... whatever it is you do. That is *not blowing anything up.*"

He laughed. Now that he was here, with nothing else to

do, perhaps he could just indulge a little and let himself learn more about the girl in front of him.

"Were you born on Earendel?" Cyan asked.

"No. I was always a station kid. Born on Kora one-ninety-two, then we moved around a lot."

"What's a lot?"

"Two moves with my family, and the last one—to Earendel—on my own."

"Is it home?"

Elaina's smile was wistful as she thought about it. "It's a place. But home, I think, is a person."

Cyan considered that, and how true he wanted it to be.

"He's very calm." Elaina smiled at Priad.

"Yeah, he's a very good boy." The warg was used to sleeping on shuttles.

"Are you calm?"

He very much wanted to be. He wanted to just relax and stop thinking... stop *doing*... sometimes. Sometimes it worked. "I'm getting there. But it's hard to turn off sometimes."

"When you speak, you seem calm," Elaina mused.

If only she knew.

"Thank you. I'm calmer around people. Some people. They help me slow down."

Elaina nodded. "Some people help me slow down too."

Cyan considered her. "Tell me about your family."

Elaina's hands went to her knees, palms smoothing the fabric of her trousers as she studied her lap.

"Both my parents were engineers. Different kinds. We were never really close."

"In what way?"

She shrugged. "Physically, emotionally. Let's just say we weren't the hugging type."

"Are you the hugging type?"

Elaina broke into a grin, finally looking back up at him. "Very much. But I don't need them," she hastened to add. "I can take care of myself."

"I like that about you."

Self-sufficiency was important. He'd been with people who clung more than he could accommodate. A certain amount of distance was good, he thought.

He told himself this even as something chewed at him—a contradiction he would need to reconcile, but not one he was interested in entertaining now.

"How long are you here for?" Elaina asked the question he'd been wondering himself.

"On Earendel?"

"On Earendel, in the quadrant... what's after your mysterious mission?"

Cyan watched her, understanding exactly what she wanted to know. Why couldn't he just say it?

"I don't know how long my work here will take. But eventually I want to find home too."

"And your home? Is it a place or a person?"

Cyan wished he could tell her what she might want to hear, but... "I think it's both. Home is somewhere on Gaia. But it's incomplete without a person—a family—to share it with."

"Makes sense." Elaina looked out the viewport. "We're almost there."

Cyan followed her gaze. The stars glowed distant and unmoving, but something was stirring out there. It was as heavy as the weight on his back. Whatever they were heading toward, it wouldn't be quiet for long.

SIXTEEN

ELAINA

THE MOMENT her boots hit the station floor, Elaina sensed that something was very wrong here. The disturbance was a shiver under her skin. She cleared her throat in the stuffy air. Filtration was definitely compromised. She'd have to take care of that first.

It almost took her mind off Cyan, disembarking behind her. He made her think in a way nobody else had before. Was it him, or was it just that she was making an effort not to shut down and let herself connect with someone? Was that what it was like?

This is trouble.

Elaina looked around, searching for the distant voices raised in frustration. First Officer Bor Petters was waiting for her at the shuttle bay exit.

"Fairan," he said, urgent. "You need to come with me."

She fell into step beside him as he led her to the bridge, trying to ignore the sudden feeling of weightlessness as she was hit by the station's artificial grav. She felt as though she would lift off, though obviously her feet were firmly planted on the floor. Each stride was lighter, longer.

Cyan's footsteps echoed behind her, along with the

languid clicking of claws on metal, occasionally punctuated by a small stumble as the warg surely also got used to the unique sensation.

They entered the primary command center, then went right through to the tech hub, where the station's systems were housed.

"The most critical thing broken right now is the ox filtration system." Bor told her what she'd already guessed. He pointed her to a terminal in the corner. "That's the debugging entry point. I've set up the access codes, but you'll need to be quick. The system's been offline for the better part of the sol."

Elaina had just landed on a station with one of the worst problems imaginable: breathable air. She glanced back at Priad, who was gazing expectantly at his master as Cyan spoke to another officer, muttering something about quarters. If she had already sensed the diminished airflow, it'd be even worse for the warg's smaller lungs. She had to get to work. Now.

Elaina plopped into the rolling seat at the terminal, tucking one foot under her thigh as she opened up the debugging datacore and plugged in, getting to work.

A few seconds later, she remembered herself.

"Hey, Bor, can we get another chair for—" She glanced over her shoulder to beckon Cyan over, only to find both him and Priad gone. She shrugged, turning back to the display in front of her. A familiar current tugged at her fingertips, and she was ready to dive into it.

―――――

HOURS LATER, the ox filtration system was pumping at optimal volumes again, and Elaina had moved through sanitation, solar shields, and radiation monitoring systems.

Unlike her last stay at the station, this time most of the damage was more... well, *graceful* was the only way to put it. Last time she was crawling all over the ship, rearranging wiring and soldering PCBs and other onboard components. Now most systems could be restored remotely, which one would think should make it easier.

It was not. Whereas physical damage was easily diagnosed and repaired, this was trickier—firmware issues. And each system she went into manifested the problems slightly differently. Each component was harder to debug, harder to repair. By the time Elaina got the critical systems back up, her brain hurt.

She rubbed her eyes and spoke into the mic installed at the comms station: "Bor, go check the airlock doors in Portside Two now. The leak should be sealed, I hope."

"Roger."

Elaina tensed at a new voice behind her: "How are you getting on?"

She turned her head slightly, speaking over her shoulder. "Good, thanks."

As Cyan approached, the warm, rich smell of spiced labba stew filled the air. The scent of slow-cooked meat, tatt roots, and a hint of earthy herbs made her stomach rumble despite the stress of the sol. She looked up as he set the containers down beside her.

Elaina had realized she'd gotten used to seeing Cyan in his armor. The white shirt that was loosely fitted around his broad torso and had a series of actual physical buttons instead of magnetic clasps made him look so casual somehow.

Elaina cleared her throat and eyed the chunks of labba marinating in the steaming bowls.

"Thanks," she said. "But I'm a vegetarian."

"Oh, right." His face fell a little.

"But I'm not that picky," she resigned despite herself. "I'll just eat all the other good stuff. Maybe Priad wants the meat?"

"You sure?" Cyan leaned on an empty spot at the bench, crossing his arms over his chest. The sleeves of that old timey shirt were rolled up to his forearms, and she noted the faded ink markings running from his wrists and underneath the fabric.

"Yeah. Thanks for getting it." She pushed her keyboard forward to make space for the bowl, and as the scent hit her once more she wondered if maybe she should reconsider her vegetarianism just this one time.

She was starving.

"Did they get you a cabin?" she asked casually, blowing on the spoonful of hot stew that she was dying to put in her mouth.

"Yes."

"Not portside, I hope. I haven't patched that airlock yet."

Also, *her* cabin was always on starboard. Not that it mattered, of course.

"Actually, yeah. They told me to clear out for a bit. But I had work to do anyway."

He said his work was about these tech glitches, and that work was being done here. By her. What other work did he mean? But it wasn't her place to ask. She barely knew the man, or what he did.

"Where's your giant sword?" she asked instead. Or was that too personal too?

Cyan turned slightly, exposing the massive weapon strapped to his left hip. It definitely did not look practical, but who was she to judge a man's sword?

"Right... I don't know that you'll need a sword here. You may as well not drag it around," she said.

Cyan adjusted it on his waist, then patted the hilt. "It remains with me always."

"*Always?*"

He arched an eyebrow. "Okay, it remains with me *almost* always."

Elaina focused on her stew.

They ate in silence, Elaina devouring her food much faster than he did—she hadn't realized how hungry she was while so focused on her work. In fact, she hadn't eaten since breakfast planetside that morning, and that was nearly a full sol ago.

"Can I give him these?" She tilted the bowl toward Cyan to display the leftover pieces of labba she didn't eat.

"Sure."

Priad's furry ears perked up when she approached him with the bowl.

"Tell him to sit first."

Elaina raised a finger and looked sternly at the warg, whose tail was now flopping back and forth enthusiastically. "Priad, *sitka.*"

The beast cocked his head to the side, tongue lolling out.

"*Sitka,*" she repeated.

Another second later, Priad's butt plopped firmly on the floor in that funny way he had, his expression unchanging as he stared between her and the bowl in her hand.

"Good boy!" Elaina praised, then looked back at Cyan, who nodded. She set the bowl on the floor, grinning as the warg tucked in with wanton enthusiasm.

"So tell me about the glitches," Cyan said once she was back in her seat, watching the screen running diagnostics on the critical systems she'd already repaired.

Elaina groaned at the red lines flicking past a sea of white and green. The ox filtration was acting up again.

"Crap," she said. "Hold on, let me look at this."

"Can I look too?"

"Sure," she said absently as she propped a foot on the chair and hunched over the keyboard.

The nape of her neck prickled as Cyan leaned over behind her to look at her screen. This was the closest they'd gotten. She hadn't noticed before, but he had a subtle spicy, woody scent to him. Elaina bit her lip and tried to focus on the display as he leaned closer and reached one arm over to prop himself against the table, bracketing her in. His breath on her skin made focusing harder than it should've been. The proximity was distracting, making her stomach flop in a way she wished she didn't like so much.

Elaina cleared her throat.

"This isn't a glitch," she said as her fingers picked over the keyboard.

"What?"

"You said to tell you about the glitches. This is not a glitch."

She navigated into the system's flux component, accessing the firmware code and scanning for the telltale signs of the pattern she'd noticed.

"Then what is it?"

"Of course." She groaned. "It's changed again. Every time it's different."

The tension in Cyan's voice was palpable. "What's different, Elaina?"

She'd noticed it before, and her initial hunch had been confirmed throughout the sol. At first it looked like random runtime code corruption. Memory addresses missing, null pointers leading to nowhere. Like something had fucked with the firmware at random. But each time she tackled a new system, the corruption grew more sophisticated. Too sophisticated to be a bug.

Elaina marveled at the way the affected code-point had been modified at runtime to inject an intermittent flux surge at escalating intervals until the system overloaded. Once she narrowed it down and excised it, bringing the ox filtration system back to optimal capacity, she leaned back in her seat, Cyan's presence even more palpable behind her. He rose and watched her, a frown knotting his brows.

"It's a virus," she said.

SEVENTEEN

CYAN

CYAN SAT across from Elaina and listened intently as she explained what she'd found, but there was something nagging at the edges of his awareness. This virus wasn't just data. It was more. It was dangerous. It was why he was here.

"It's been changing. Almost like..." Elaina hesitated.

"Go on," Cyan instructed quietly.

"Almost like it's being modified. But there's no way. I checked the access logs—nobody but me's been in these systems for spans." She frowned.

"Spans?"

"Umm..." She looked up, searching for words. "A set of seven sols."

Right. Weeks.

"Go on," he nodded.

"So it must be programmed to self-modify somehow," she continued. "But it's... The sophistication, it's like..."

He sensed the weight of what was on the tip of her awareness, the thing that her rational mind wouldn't let her say. Probably wouldn't even let her think.

But *he* could think it. And he could say it for her.

"It's evolving."

Elaina chuckled. "That's a little too anthropomorphizing for my tastes."

"But you know it's true."

"How do *you* know it's true?"

"I feel it."

"What does that mean?" But he saw it in her eyes. She felt it too. She just wouldn't let herself believe it.

Cyan leaned forward, gently unwinding her arms. He traced down her forearms until her hands were wrapped in his own, and pulled her closer in her chair.

"Not everything can be explained with logic, Elaina," he said quietly, eyes locked on hers.

She nipped at her bottom lip in that way she did when she was thinking. She had to stop thinking.

He pulled her forward, closing the distance between them as he captured her lips with his own, cutting off her surprised gasp. Hot breath washed over his cheek and a quiet groan caught in his throat as her hands unwound from him to prop on his knees at either side of her, seeking balance. Warmth filled his chest, expanding through his limbs. He gripped her upper arms, squeezing more tightly than he'd intended as he deepened the kiss, and she parted her mouth for him, permitting him to take a taste, their tongues brushing together with dangerous curiosity.

Cyan broke the contact before things went any further, but the tension between them didn't dissipate. It hung in the air like an unfinished conversation. Her mouth parted slightly, her pupils large as she tucked a strand of hair behind her ear. She watched his mouth.

He'd intended the kiss to interrupt her racing mind, but he couldn't pretend something between them hadn't shifted. She'd let him in, more than just physically. He could see it in her eyes, in the way her body had relaxed into him so easily. Too easily.

He realized how close he was to stepping over a line he had no business crossing with a woman he just met on a planet he'd never stay on once his job was done. Not that he'd never had casual company like that before, but he had a feeling that wasn't the right thing here, with her.

The weight at his side grew more insistent, a reminder of the task ahead. Cyan couldn't afford this. Not when something so much bigger was at stake. Whatever was happening here, it would have to wait.

"I need to find out where it's coming from," he said, his voice steady despite the storm brewing inside him. "And I need to stop it."

EIGHTEEN

ELAINA

THEY HAD PARTED ways in the station's main hall, veering into the directions of their respective cabins.

Elaina realized she'd been thinking about kissing him, on and off, since their lunch date. Mostly off, considering she hadn't let herself get her hopes up when he said he'd contact her and then proceeded to drop off the face of Earendel.

But now, maybe things could go somewhere. They were on this station together, hunting the same mystery, and... Well, his brain just clicked in all the right ways somehow.

Chill. It's only a kiss.

Cyan was very likeable, and it seemed like they might want the same things. But Elaina didn't yet know that they'd want them with each other. She needed more time with him to know that.

And now maybe she'd have her chance to find out.

He said he wanted to live on Gaia eventually. The ancient birthplace of humanity. It was an artifact and had maintained many old traditions for the sake of keeping them. The language would take time to learn.

But Elaina was usually a fast learner.

A wave of fondness came over her. Not thinking twice about it for once, she smiled to herself and subvocalized a message:

I think you're great.

That wasn't too forward, was it? Or would it scare him off? She'd said things like that before, but only to people who were safe. Those she'd known would return the sentiment. With Cyan, he was practically a stranger, whose timing was unreliable at best. What if he never even replied? What if she misread him completely, and the rest of their stay on the station would be super awkward? What if she liked him, and he didn't care much at all?

But maybe the best things just needed a little bit more faith—how would she ever experience them if she didn't take a chance?

"Send," she issued the command vocally, her voice defying her second thoughts.

━━━━━━

THANKFULLY, the coffee dispensers at the station's canteen had not yet been affected by the mysterious virus. Elaina yawned as she picked up her carboform cup of old station grind.

Coffee was possibly Earth's most cherished export. Sometimes even more so than humanity itself. Elaina sipped, not caring that it burned the tip of her tongue, as she walked in the direction of the primary command center.

"Any news in the diagnostics overnight?" she asked Bor when he answered her chime.

"Seems good for now. None of the systems you repaired

yesterday have declined yet, but we still got heat and comms down in parts of the station."

"I'll take care of those today," Elaina said. "When's the backup tech coming?"

Being the one the entire station relied on to keep its critical systems up and running was a point of pride, but Elaina couldn't do this indefinitely, especially with back-to-back shifts disorienting her system. She pressed her fingers just below her sternum, massaging away the subtle heaviness there.

"A few sols, they say. Do you know what's causing it yet?"

"A virus," she said. "Highly sophisticated and evolv... self-modifying."

"Shit. Sabotage."

"I don't know yet, but it's something. I'm still gathering data."

"All right, just get here quick. I'm seeing lots of new red that just appeared on these screens of yours."

Elaina sighed, cutting the connection. It was going to be a long few sols until her replacement arrived.

In the little debugging and diagnostics room, Elaina settled back in her seat and began her work. Once again, the next time she plugged into an affected system, she found the virus had mutated.

"What *are* you?" she muttered absently as she excised the affected code. The deeper she went, the more the truth of what Cyan had said sank in, and it unsettled her to her core. She wasn't just hunting down a virus someone had deployed. She was hunting an entity—an animal all its own.

And she had this off-axis feeling that the animal was toying with her.

Elaina shook her head, batting away the thought. The virus was clever in so far as it was cleverly programmed. To evolve, sure. But software could evolve. Open-ended simulations had been the stuff of theories and experiments for forever, all the way from humanity's simplistic Gaian origins.

This virus mutated so quickly, ever-learning. And somehow, it knew just how to slip under her defenses. Elaina had debugged thousands of systems in her career, but never like this. She didn't really want to admit it, but she almost admired it.

"But what do you want..." Elaina muttered at her screen.

"Is it saying anything?"

Elaina jumped at the voice behind her, her focus shattered. The pang of irritation subsided immediately when she saw Cyan at her side, once more with two steaming food boxes.

"No," Elaina said sheepishly. "I'm just talking to myself."

"I brought you some lunch." Cyan set a portion of baked river snake and beans at the desk before her.

Elaina stared at it in confusion.

"I'm a vegetarian," she said. Again. She'd told him, and yet he kept offering her meat. Why?

"Fuck, I'm sorry. I forgot."

"It's all right." Elaina picked up the fork in the bowl. "The beans look great."

And the nymph smelled disappointingly delicious. Maybe just a bite?

Vegetarianism wasn't an uncommon diet, anywhere in the known universe except for some purely carnivorous communities borne out of necessity in locations that had no edible plant life. Gaia certainly was not one of those.

Stop finding issues. Things are crazy around here. It's an honest mistake.

And just the fact that he even came over with food was considerate.

When a tiny bit of soft nymph meat crumbled off the chunk, she surreptitiously let it fall onto her fork, and subsequently into her mouth.

Priad got the rest.

———

"I LIKED YOUR PING," Cyan said once she was done. "I think you're great too."

"Hmm?" Elaina pretended to have forgotten. "Oh! That one." She focused on her terminal. "Thank you."

"Do you want to have dinner with me?"

She glanced at the cool, steady silver of his gaze, watching. Waiting. "Yes. What time?"

Cyan drummed his fingers beside her on the desk. They were nice fingers. "I've got some stuff to check out here, but I'll ping you soon, when I know when I'll be done."

"Sounds good." Elaina spotted a red diagnostics line on her screen from the corner of her eye, and already her attention was being drawn back to the virus. Her nemesis. "I hope you learn something we can use."

He nodded. "Me too. You'll catch me up on your stuff here?"

"Sure. Thanks for lunch." Elaina smiled, letting her eyes linger on him for a second before delving back into her debugger.

NINETEEN

CYAN

HE SAT on the bed in his cabin, the sword splayed across his knees. He traced its glow, which had grown more persistent. The vein cleaving down the blade now emitted a faint crimson light continuously through the day. The blade was growing restless.

Cyan glanced at Priad, curled up protectively at the cabin door. They were close. Coming up to orbit had been the right decision.

He slid the blade into its sheath. He'd spent the day interviewing people on the station, and they had grown suspicious of his purpose here. He was no officer. No official. He was just a tagalong who came with their astrotechnician. But he did extract *some* useful information, like the dockman's logs with names of all incoming and outgoing transports, as well as more details about the station's purpose.

Earendel's orbital station served as a gateway for incoming traders and other visitors, many of whom could sell their wares without even bothering to set foot planetside. It was a sentinel command hub watching over the planet below, as well as controlling the solar farm that would then siphon energy to Chevron City. A sort of industrial and trading outpost.

The gravity on the station was not synchronized to the planet, and he could tell it affected Priad. Cyan himself adjusted quickly, getting used to a subtly modified gait in the lighter weight.

Elaina's ping the night before both moved and concerned him. The compliment itself was trivial, but he could tell it meant something to her. Cyan stared at the sword in its sheath.

She didn't even speak Gaian. She was so different from everything he had envisioned for himself.

But there was a fire in her that touched him, and a tentative naivety he almost wished he could share. She was a storm of subtle contradictions. Controlled—a little too much, but with bursts of excitement where that slipped. He could see it in the way her eyes lit up when she spoke about her work or looked at Priad. It was in the way she moved, as though constantly pulling herself back to more appropriately constrained composure. There was a lust for existence beneath her quiet aloofness, one he couldn't quite put a finger on but wanted to understand.

It was late, but he was ready.

I'm free now. Come?

He sent the ping and lay back on the bed, tucking his hands behind his head as he stilled his mind.

Sorry, I hadn't heard from you and made other plans.

He frowned, then another ping came in:

Meet me at the observation deck?

TWENTY

ELAINA

THE CURVED viewport dominated the small observation deck, Earendel's surface stretching endlessly below. Elaina sat cross-legged on the worn cushions of the viewing bench, close enough to Cyan to feel his warmth but not quite touching. She'd been up there with her food after her shift, staring out at the planet and the nebula.

"It's different seeing it from up here," she said, watching backlit rainbow dust storms swirl across Earendel's surface. "Makes you realize how small everything is."

"Does that bother you?"

"No. I think it's comforting, actually. The perspective." She traced patterns in the cushion's fabric. "When you're planetside, it's easy to get caught up in... everything. Up here, you can see how temporary it all is."

Cyan hummed, his eyes still fixed on the view. The sword lay across his lap, ever-present. She wondered if he slept with it.

"How serious were you?" she asked carefully, keeping her tone academic. "About returning to Gaia someday?"

"I think about it often." His answer was measured. "But duty tends to have other plans."

"Right." She pulled her knees to her chest. "I used to think I'd know when I found the right place to stay. That it would just... click. But maybe that's not how it works."

"I've been thinking about what you said before," he said quietly. "About home being a person."

"And?"

"It's complicated when that person also feels like a project scope conflict."

Elaina's heart lurched, but she kept her voice steady. "I think when you find the right research partner, you'd know. The way your minds just... sync up. But timing is important in any collaboration. Both parties have to be ready to commit."

"And what if one party's existing commitments conflict with the project parameters?" His voice was quiet.

"Then you'd need to evaluate priorities. Determine if the potential results justify restructuring prior obligations." She stared hard at the planet below. "Hypothetically speaking."

The silence stretched between them. Finally, Cyan shifted beside her.

"I should feed Priad," he said, rising. "He gets restless when his routine is disrupted."

"Of course." Elaina smiled. "Wouldn't want to neglect your partner."

He hesitated, looking down at her. For a moment she thought he might say more. Instead, he simply nodded and walked away, leaving her alone with the stars.

She pressed her forehead to the cool glass of the viewport, watching his reflection fade. They were both overthinking this. But maybe that was safer than the alternative.

When the ping came, she knew who it was from.

Have dinner with me tomorrow. 3000, my
cabin?

Elaina bit her lip through a smile as she subvocalized a
response:

A time AND a place? See you then.

TWENTY-ONE
ELAINA

THE STATION'S warning klaxon faded as Elaina crawled through the service shaft, following flickering emergency lights. A failing airlock shouldn't be surprising—this was the third today. But something about this one felt different.

Sweat dripped down her neck as she lowered herself from the open panel onto the floor below. Her hands were already trembling from muscle fatigue after the previous two repairs. She pressed the pressure gauge to the read slot at the side of the massive airlock door, its internals splayed open before her. With her other hand, she stretched the calibrator into the mechanism, the door's corroded inner edges snagging her sleeve as she reached deeper.

The readouts matched the pattern from the other doors —that same fingerprint she was starting to recognize all too well. Only this time it had manifested with pressure instead of power fluctuations, like the virus was learning, adapting.

"Come on," she muttered, arms shaking as she tried to hold the gauge steady while reaching for the realignment seal with the calibrator. She needed a third hand—or signifi-cantly more upper body strength—to manage this alone.

Heavy boots echoed behind her. "Everything all right?"

She didn't look back at Cyan, no time to question why he was even there. "This seal's stuck. I need to realign it while holding pressure constant, but I can't..." She grunted as her grip slipped again. "Can't get enough leverage."

"What do you need?"

"Just... hold this." She gestured with her elbow toward the pressure gauge. "Keep it at exactly this angle while I work the calibrator."

Cyan took over the gauge, and Elaina breathed a sigh of relief as her straining shoulder got a break. She gave herself a moment to shake out her newly free hand before reaching into the hatch to tweak the calibrator against the internal mechanism.

But her tired hands got clumsy. She swore under her breath as her grip slipped and the readout on the gauge plummeted. The warning klaxon screamed back to life as oxygen began venting rapidly from the other side.

Then came the pounding—desperate, frantic hits against metal. Elaina and Cyan exchanged horrified glances.

"There's someone in there."

"Shit." The blood drained from Elaina's face as she scrambled to get the calibrator back in position. Her fingers trembled against the mechanism, each failed attempt punctuated by another terrified bang from inside.

"Steady," Cyan told her. "You've got this."

But she didn't. Her arms were leaden from the strain of climbing, then stretching into the hatch. She finally locked onto the seal, but it wouldn't budge. The gauge's warning light pulsed an angry red as pressure continued to drop.

"I think it's stuck," she gritted through her teeth. The pounding grew more erratic, desperate. How much air was left in there?

"Elaina." Her eyes snapped to his, his gaze so calm despite everything. "Breathe. I said you've got this."

She swallowed, nodding, and took a deep, shaky breath. "Again."

She closed her eyes, tuning out the banging as she got herself steady. "Okay."

Slowly her grip stabilized and she was able to apply enough pressure to twist the calibrator in its seal. She kept her eyes closed. "Pressure?"

"Creeping up. It's working."

She nodded and continued to twist gradually, keeping the motion stable. "Tell me when it moves up to one-oh-one kilopascals."

"I will."

A few more seconds of painstaking adjustment and Cyan gave her the sign. "All right, it's there. You're good."

Elaina released a shaky sigh and extracted the calibrator from the hatch. Her arm had been marked with bloody scratches where it had snagged on various components.

"It's okay," she said preemptively when Cyan's gaze fell on the marks. "We've gotta keep going, open the door while the pressure holds."

That was easier said than done, with the airlock mechanism completely disengaged. It would have to be pulled open manually.

"Let's hope the backup gets here soon enough," Elaina shook her head.

"I'll do it."

"Cyan, these doors need, like, three people."

But he was already grabbing the heavy latch and forcing it down, metal creaking under the force. Once dislodged, he yanked the lock latch toward him once, twice, forcing it into unlocked position.

"Step back."

Elaina did as he said, giving him space as he grabbed the holdbar with both hands and leaned back with it, starting to pull.

His back heaved, tendons of the neck straining under the force as he hauled the slab. Elaina fought the urge to jump in and help, sensing she would only distract him. And slowly, slowly, the mass of the airlock door budged, and a small arm reached through the opening.

She scurried toward it, taking the girl's hand.

"You're okay," Elaina said. "We'll get you out."

Then the door screeched another few inches, just enough for the girl to slip out.

"Asana!" a shaken voice called behind them, and the girl ran past Elaina into the woman's arms.

Cyan was already pushing, sealing the airlock shut once more before ox began to leak. Backup had arrived, two men pounding down the hall to help seal the thing shut.

When it was done, Cyan bent over with his arms on his knees, catching his breath.

"Thank you," the woman said, still clutching the girl. "We didn't realize this section was locked down for repairs..."

Elaina barely heard the explanation that followed. She glanced at Cyan, but he was focused on checking the seal one final time.

"Thank you," she came up behind him, resting a hand on his shoulder. "Are you okay?"

"Yes. I'm good. You?"

"Yeah, but I should get back," she said. "Two more to check."

Cyan straightened. "I'll help."

Elaina started to refuse, tell him she could handle it. But the words died in her throat—clearly she could use the help.

"Thank you." She grabbed her toolkit, wincing at her scratched arm. "That'd be great."

As they headed toward the next failing lock, Elaina's dataslate pinged with another alert. She pulled it out, frowning at the readout. The virus's signature was changing again.

She'd have to figure that out later. Right now she had repairs to make, and for once she wasn't making them alone.

TWENTY-TWO

CYAN

WHEN ELAINA SHOWED up at his cabinstep after the shift that night, he'd already had dinner prepared and Priad fed with a portion of kobalin steak. They'd tried to give him hound food, but Priad needed real meat, not reconstituted synthetic protein.

The cabin was small, and the only seating aside from the bed was an uncomfortable-looking rolling chair. Elaina made for the chair.

"Vegetables this time," Cyan handed her her portion.

Her eyes lit up with an unguarded smile. "Thank you!"

The Earendel-native root vegetables looked odd to Cyan's eye. Misshapen fingerlike things that were tough in texture but gave off a satisfying savory tang. The stuff on the side he recognized from planetside: sandseeds. A favorite snack of the locals. The misleadingly tough outer shells, while edible, were only a facade for the nectar within.

"Thanks for the assist today," Elaina said.

"How's your arm?" Cyan glanced at the synthetic paste spread smoothly over her cuts.

"Oh. it's all patched. I've had worse." She grinned.

They talked over dinner, Cyan sitting on the edge of his

bed and Elaina in the chair across from him. When Priad strolled over to sit between them Elaina reached down to scratch his neck absently. Priad liked her. Cyan liked her too.

He needed to get her closer.

"When did you leave Gaia?" Elaina had been asking him about his home.

"When I was eighteen, I went to study at the Martian colony. Moved around a few stations since then, but didn't leave the galaxy until I started... this work."

Elaina's eyes fell on the sword in its holster next to him. "With that?"

"Yes."

She continued brushing Priad's fur, but there was a careful tension in her posture. Her eyes flicked to the weapon once more. Her next question came cautiously. "Can you tell me more?"

The full extent of the sword's story was not something Cyan generally revealed to people, especially as most would probably find it esoteric and weird. And Elaina's work, seemingly her entire life on Earendel, seemed centered around hard sciences. But he had an idea.

"This might be a long story," he said. "Come sit here, that chair doesn't deserve you."

"It really isn't very comfortable," Elaina conceded with a small smile. Cyan moved over, making more room on the bed. She sat with a few inches of space between them. Still distant—cautious, or uninterested?

"Okay." She leaned against the wall and stretched out her legs, clasping her hands together between her thighs. "Ready for the long story."

TWENTY-THREE

CYAN

THE OLD WORLD Forest wrapped tight around him, black branches creaking overhead. Seventeen years old, and Cyan thought he knew these woods. He'd grown up climbing their ancient trees, racing Faera through clearings choked with ferns. The forest had been his escape when his father's brief visits home filled the house with that familiar tension—his mother's tight smiles, the careful dance of two people who'd forgotten how to exist in the same space.

That morning had been especially bad. His father, home for three sols between trading missions, had tried to discuss Cyan's acceptance to the Martian Academy over breakfast. Mother's fork had clinked against her plate with each mention of space travel, her eyes drifting to some distant point. They all still carried the image of Kern's ship exploding in the night sky the year before, how it had lit up Gaia like a second sun. His cousin had been accepted to the academy too. A once in a lifetime chance. He'd chosen to go, eager not to miss his shot at the universe, despite rumors of the ship's warp drive malfunction.

"You have a choice to make," his father had said gruffly,

but his eyes were already far away, like he was halfway back to the stars. Always choosing anywhere but home.

Mother's fingertips whitened around her glass. Twenty years of similar choices lined her eyes. Some choices, once made, carved permanent paths. The Martian Academy's acceptance felt like lead in Cyan's pocket now. They all pretended not to notice how his hands shook whenever anyone mentioned space travel.

A gust of wind stirred the canopy, sending dappled shadows dancing across the forest floor. Something glinted among the roots of a massive oak—a flash of something that shouldn't be there. Cyan approached carefully. The tree's roots had grown around whatever lay buried, creating a natural cradle of twisted wood.

He squatted low on his haunches, brushing away layers of dead leaves. His young, delicate fingers met cool steel.

The sword's hilt emerged first, then the broad blade as he carefully extracted it from its earthen bed. It was unlike any blade he'd seen in the settlement's museum of pre-Reju-venation artifacts. The metal was a dark ash, almost black, with a jagged vein of gold running its length. It hummed in his grip, a subtle vibration that seeped into his bones.

"What are you?" he whispered.

The sword's weight settled into his palms like it belonged there. Like it had been waiting. A certainty washed over Cyan—this wasn't just some relic. This was so much more. Destiny perhaps, reaching out to him through centuries of soil and roots, offering something greater than the paralysis of choice, something stronger than his father's wavering commitment or his cousin's fatal decision.

Cyan's mind quieted. The endless churn of what-ifs fell away. He rose, the blade steady in his grip. The forest around him seemed to hold its breath. Countless paths stretched before him through the ancient trees, but for the first time in his life, he knew exactly where to go. The acceptance letter in his pocket didn't feel quite so heavy anymore.

The sword would guide him. All he had to do was trust in its pull, let it lead him where he needed to be. No more uncertainty. No more watching people choose to leave.

Cyan turned toward home. The trees whispered around him, speaking to him like they always had, but he was already learning not to listen. His fate—the only thing he had to listen to—was gripped tightly in his hands.

"WHEN THE SWORD claimed me I was not yet fully ready for everything it had wanted me to see," Cyan said after telling her the story of his discovery in the Northern wilds.

He'd said more than he had intended. She'd been skeptical about the concept of fate before. What would she think of him now?

He had watched Elaina's face intently for the skepticism he was so sure would come.

Instead, she asked, "What did it want you to see?"

Something unwound in Cyan's chest at Elaina's unfazed acceptance of his story—a pit that had been there, tying his tongue to stay grounded to objective reality. Cyan realized it only when it began to ease, but that pit was older than this conversation.

"You're amazing." The words were blurted out before he thought them through.

There was that smile again, nearly so disarming as to make him miss the fact that she had shifted closer to him, just a finger now separating their thighs. The air between them was charged with unspoken affection. Her fingers moved slightly, tracing circles in the fabric of her leggings. Cyan's hand moved almost on its own to cover hers, feeling the warmth of her smooth skin beneath his rough fingers. They were no longer delicate like the ones that had picked up the blade in those woods.

TWENTY-FOUR

ELAINA

THEY WERE CLOSE ENOUGH for her to feel Cyan's breath skirting down her cheek as she looked down at their intertwined hands. The heaviness she'd been feeling since her last stint up at the station was gone, replaced by a weightless charge enveloping the space around them. Anticipation coiled tight as Cyan's breathing deepened next to her, his thumb tracing circles in the back of her hand.

Tilting her face toward him, Elaina whispered, "What did the sword want you to—"

He captured her lips before she could finish, taking the underlying invitation. Electricity zinged to her head and down her spine as she leaned into the kiss, turning toward him as he turned toward her. Leaning into him as he leaned into her, a magnet and a mirror. He brought his free hand to her face, enveloping her cheek in the heat of his palm. A strained sound left her throat as his tongue nudged at the seam of her mouth, and she complied, parting her lips.

Cyan's kiss was not shy—he deepened it, leading the exploration of their tongues, and Elaina took the chance to nip at his lower lip, tasting him. The soft grunt the bite elicited made her clench, her hips shifting instinctively as she turned further into him.

"Spread your legs a little for me," Cyan's voice was hoarse against her lips, and her body reacted before her brain could, her thighs parting. He untwined his hand from hers to slide it gently to her thigh, the light pressure raising chills on her skin. He leaned his forehead against hers, lips hovering a sliver away, so close she could still taste him, as his hand stroked her inner thighs.

"I like when you tell me what to do," Elaina swallowed, her eyes glued down to his mouth, a little blurry in its proximity.

Something shifted in the energy between them. The thought of giving herself to him completely, relinquishing control, pooled between her legs. This wasn't just about following his lead—it was about letting herself trust in whatever happened next.

"Come here," he rasped.

His hold on her cheek hardened and he tilted her face up for a forceful kiss as his other hand traveled to the apex between her legs. She gasped as he finally touched her, lightly at first, then harder, and then it was gone as he gripped her hip instead and shifted them both, dragging her on top of him.

Heat spread across her skin like plainsfire, every nerve ending sparking under his hands. Her breath caught as she slid against him, taut with need. The air was heady with the scent of his skin—a mix of leather, musk, and something uniquely Cyan. Every shift of his body beneath hers sent the sound of rustling fabric through the weighted silence in the tiny cabin, punctuating their uneven breathing.

Her knees planted on either side of his waist, her hands finding their way on their own up his sides. His fingers laced at the nape of her neck, pulling her face toward him, his hips coming up against hers, longing through layers of fabric. He took her hand and guided it down between them.

"Feel that," he said, groaning as she pressed her hand to the hardness through his trousers. "Feel what you did."

Elaina choked on a moan, the quiet, steady words burrowing into her core.

"I did that?" She glanced down. She wanted to hear it again.

"Mmhmm," he said. "You did."

Elaina shifted herself against him, her body feeling like it was ready to unseal, to open wide and let him in. Her blood pumped with newfound urgency, rushing in her ears like a power surge building to overload as she brought her mouth to his cheek, down his jaw, to his neck. She wanted to devour him. She wanted to *be* devoured.

Slow down, alarm bells tried to make her see reason. It was too soon. She barely knew him. She wasn't ready.

But she wanted this.

"Do you want to get on your knees?" Cyan muttered, stroking a lock of hair behind her ear as her lips and tongue explored his collarbone, her back arched up over him, her hands roaming.

"Yes," she breathed. She was practically salivating at the thought. That, she *was* ready for.

"Good."

How could one word make her melt so completely? She let him shift her down to the floor as he pushed himself up on his elbows. Cyan grabbed the pillow from his bed and put it down for her knees.

"Thank you." She smiled up at him, positioning herself between his splayed legs. She trailed her hands down his shirt, fiddling with the archaic Gaian button-clasping system. He helped, his rugged fingers replacing her own to give her access to his abdomen. The salty musk of his skin seeped onto her tongue as she tasted the trail of his stomach, her hands lowering to tuck her fingers into his waistband.

He helped with the clasps on that too, and Elaina tugged his trousers down below his hips, her stomach flipping with anticipation.

When his shaft sprung free from its restraints, Elaina's hands and tongue gravitated to its hard heat. Cyan grasped the back of her hair, firmly staying her impatient momentum. She lingered before him, so close, and so hungry.

"Look at me when you put me in your mouth."

A fresh wave of heat coursed through her and she obeyed, her gaze locking onto his. The intensity of his stare pinned her in place, as if he were reading every inch of her soul, not just her body. His eyes darkened, and she felt herself falling—into him, into the moment, into something she couldn't control and really didn't want to.

Cyan was a storm looming over her. His brow furrowed and his expression was firm even as he nodded his approval. She opened her mouth as he stroked a thumb along her bottom lip and moaned in response to the small smile he had deemed to grant. Finally, his hand on the back of her head guided her to her destination.

Elaina's eyes nearly closed when she finally tasted him, the head sliding between her lips, but her eyes quickly flew open and back up at the firm words from above: "Eyes up here. Look at me."

He pushed her lower, forcing her to spread her knees wider on the floor to get down, looking up as she took him deeper in her mouth. The single-minded focus in his eyes was life itself, and Elaina moaned as his hips came forward to meet her. Her lips curled around his shaft on the flat of her tongue and she took him as deep as she could manage—not deep enough—and then moved back.

"Fuck," the curse escaped him as his hips began to find a

rhythm. She matched his pace, gripping his bare thighs, eager fingers digging into thick skin. Her belly tightened when he tangled his fingers roughly in her hair, bringing her forward, his breaths growing ragged.

Elaina couldn't take it anymore. She withdrew, a trail of saliva linking the head of his shaft with her lower lip. Elaina took a beat to catch her breath before choking out her request: "May I touch myself?"

The smile that lit his face was a wildfire that made her insides pool between her legs.

I would kill for that smile.

The unbidden thought chilled her so suddenly that she was sure he must've noticed. Her heart raced, not just from arousal, but from the terrifying prospect of the realization. She barely knew him, but it really felt like she meant it.

"Are you okay?" Cyan brought her back, his grip in her hair turning into something gentler. She nodded, but he pulled her up higher on her knees, bending down to tilt her chin up and still her sudden hesitation with a kiss.

"Yes," Elaina swallowed. "I'm okay."

"Good. Then yes…" The kiss turned harder then, more decisive. Cyan's tongue explored her mouth like he owned it and then he withdrew, forcing her to look at him. "You can touch yourself."

That was enough to push aside whatever distraction her brain had begun to concoct, and Elaina brought herself back down. She slid an eager hand between her thighs and her mouth back in its place on Cyan's cock, stars flaring behind her eyes as pleasure twisted from her clit and through her body like a live wire. She quickly remembered herself, opening her eyes to look at him.

"Fuck yes, just like that." Cyan bared his teeth in a concentrated scowl. She watched him watch her, his attention pinning her in place and driving her dangerously close to the edge as she felt him swell further with every increasingly haphazard thrust. Elaina's finger quickened on her clit, rubbing impatient circles, her thighs trembling with each ripple of pleasure skittering through her body. And when Cyan grabbed her face in both of his, his thumbs stroking the hair back from her temples for a better look at her eyes, Elaina felt herself start to break open.

"Cwunicumm?" She mumbled through her full mouth, his pace unrelenting, and something in the wicked grin that twisted his face told her he liked that.

"What was that? I didn't hear you," Cyan bit back.

Elaina pleaded with her eyes, begging for him to just give her this. "Cw—cwun—I—swum?" She tried again, eliciting a joyful laugh from the man fucking her mouth.

"Yes." He nodded at her—her favorite motion and apparently her new favorite word. "Yes, you can come."

That was all she needed. Elaina moaned his name indecipherably and began to come apart.

TWENTY-FIVE

CYAN

WATCHING her eyes roll back as she came with him in her mouth was the last straw. A low growl ripped out of him as he stared at her crumpling form writhe in ecstasy and yet still so dedicated to doing her job, sucking at his shaft. He fell forward over her, planting his hands on her splayed thighs as he squeezed his eyes shut and thrust himself home inside her eager mouth. He tightened as pent-up release built up inside him, his heart hammering through his ribs like a pounding war drum.

He didn't register that the roar he was hearing was his own as he emptied himself inside her mouth, his hands digging into the soft thighs underneath him. Her tongue and throat worked as she swallowed him through wet, mumbling moans.

Once spent, all air and energy rushed out of him in a flood. Cyan sighed and collapsed backward, dragging Elaina off her knees and onto the bed beside him, where she lay dazed on her stomach. He panted as he caught his breath and waited for his heart to steady, but it just kept racing.

What if it never got steady again?

"Do you want to stay?" he mumbled, bringing one arm over his eyes and splaying the other on the small of her back.

She muttered a yes, tucking herself closer against him, and he was glad.

Cyan drifted for a while, fingers luxuriating in the soft skin of the woman at his side as his mind drifted through nothing in particular. Drifting felt good.

His foot nudged something when he moved. The cool hilt of the sword at the edge of the bed. For a moment the world had been just them—her soft breathing, her warmth beside him. Would this ever be enough?

Cyan turned to the side and scooped Elaina against his chest, enjoying the weight of her head on his arm. He pushed the sword from his mind, for just a little while longer.

CYAN WOKE SLOWLY, Elaina's warmth pressed against him. For a moment, he didn't move, lying still as his mind gradually returned to the present. Her soft breaths tickled his chest, and her body at his side was somehow very familiar despite this being her first time in his bed.

Soon enough, equally-familiar restlessness crept in. It was a string pulled taut beneath his skin.

You need to move.

Cyan gently untangled himself from Elaina, trying not to wake her. She shifted, half-asleep, mumbling something incoherent.

He liked the way she mumbled. Cyan smirked to himself.

"Stay in bed," he murmured, planting a light kiss on her temple. "I'll get us something to eat."

Elaina didn't open her eyes, just nodded against the

pillow, her body curling into the spot he'd vacated. He watched her for a second longer, then grabbed his dataslate, shouldered the sword, and clicked his fingers for Priad. The warg lifted his head and followed him out of the cabin.

The station was quiet this early, but Cyan felt none of its stillness. Aimless agitation hummed just beneath his skin. He'd thought after last night—after everything—maybe he'd feel closer. That the uncertainty gnawing at him would dissipate. But now, in the cold light of morning, he felt farther from certainty than ever.

He walked down the corridor, stopping at a seat just outside the commissary. Maybe he could catch up on some work before the day began. There was time, with Elaina still sleeping. Priad's silver stare tracked his every move as Cyan turned on his dataslate and pulled up the station access logs he'd received earlier.

He scrolled through them, noting the comings and goings of the past few weeks. All uninteresting, but he could feel *something* was there to be found. The list of names, transport entries, and exit times blurred in his mind. He just had to look harder. Cyan began his search from the beginning, going through each row of arrivals and departures methodically.

He paused on his third scroll-through. Something looked off. Scrolling to the bottom of the list again, he realized a row was missing. Earendel did not get many visitors, and neither did its orbital station. There had been sixteen logged arrivals and nineteen departures in the prior six cycles.

Only that wasn't true. Just a few minutes ago, there had been *seventeen* logged arrivals. He was sure of it.

Where did that other log go? Cyan's frown deepened as he refreshed the file, to no avail. A log line had simply disappeared.

The ping startled him out of his thoughts. Elaina.

Morning! I'm up. You coming?

He stared at the message, hesitating over the screen. He hadn't been gone that long yet, plenty of time to finish this. Cyan shifted in his seat, turning his attention back to the access data and feeling the comfortable heaviness of the sword at his back. This was important. He was on to something.

WHEN CYAN finally returned to the cabin with food and coffee an hour and a half later, he was elated. He hadn't figured out the disappearance of the log, but at least he'd found a lead.

But as soon as he opened the door, his excitement drained.

The bed was empty, neatly made. He stared at the vacant space where Elaina had been barely more than an hour ago.

His heart gave an uncomfortable lurch. She hadn't waited. And why would she?

This was probably a good thing anyway. They both had work to do. Not all the station's systems were back online yet, and clearly Elaina was the only one on site capable of patching things up until he got to the root of the issue.

Cyan's hand tightened around the dataslate still in his grasp, his mind replaying the message she'd sent.

Morning! I'm up. You coming?

It hadn't seemed urgent when she'd sent it. He'd thought there was time. But now, standing in his empty cabin, it felt like a question that demanded an answer he wasn't sure he could give.

TWENTY-SIX

ELAINA

SHE HUNCHED OVER THE CONSOLE, fingers drumming against the surface as the diagnostics blazed on her screen. Her stomach rumbled, a bitter reminder of how long she'd waited for Cyan to return with the breakfast he'd promised. She should've known better. He'd done this before—disappeared after she thought they'd had an amazing time. This time just felt different. It always did, didn't it? Elaina let out a shaky breath. Maybe he was just busy. Or maybe it really was all in her head.

She had to get herself out of this situation and not treat it like some kind of fucking challenge. She'd tried to be more open, more forthcoming, and she simply picked the wrong person to do it with. Caring was presence, and reliability. It wasn't... whatever this was.

Only something about it felt so familiar. She'd never acted like *this* with a partner, but she sensed a similar uncertainty in Cyan as her own in the past, with others. Cycles-long relationships in which she never really let herself get too close.

Or maybe it was all in her head, and the perceived

relatability was just an excuse for her to tolerate this waste of time. She had to stop now, before she got too attached.

Oh, who was she kidding? She was already too attached. To a stupid stranger who was barely ever there. Who might not even like her.

Fuck. There were so many more important things to worry about. Elaina turned back to the code, scanning line after line of garbled data. At least here, in the quiet of her workstation, everything had its place. Everything made sense. Losing herself in the data was a comfort. Here, she could make progress and patch things.

Elaina's eyes narrowed as a strange pattern flashed across the screen. She paused, scrolling back. There it was again—a ping from a system she didn't recognize.

"What the dead drift is acorn one-oh-nine?" she muttered as if the ghost in the machine could hear her.

She dived into the diagnostics, and that only made the confusion worse. The firmware for this thing wasn't written in any code she could recognize. Elaina fumbled about as best she could, deducing what was going on... She found something somewhat familiar eventually, a locator driver connected haphazardly to the foreign code. That, at least, was a lead—the locator had been a common gadget used to track high-value devices across the station. Elaina had patched dozens of them up here. And this one appeared to be stationed somewhere in the decommission dock.

But what is it tracking?

Elaina wheeled herself back from the console, spinning around in her chair, her mind spinning with it. She needed a breakthrough. If she couldn't figure out where this virus came from, how was she ever going to stop it? Earendel was barely on anyone's radar. No one was coming to save them. And she couldn't even keep her own head straight, let alone patch this mess. Was this foreign system related, or a false flare taking her on a ghost run?

She tried to think, but her brain wouldn't work and a headache was threatening at the back of her skull. She rubbed her sternum, thinking. Elaina knew she wouldn't be able to keep this up for long. She was already on an irregular orbital stint and it had already taken her way too long to recover after the last one. It was just getting so hard to connect the dots.

The realization hit her like a decommissioned satellite crashing into the sand dunes.

Of course!

This was why she'd gotten so weirdly tangled up in Cyan. She was still messed up from orbit, and now she was back in it. Elaina simply wasn't thinking straight, her head all over the place. She wasn't making good decisions—fixating on a near stranger, likely exaggerating whatever connection she'd sensed, and, in retrospect, catastrophizing his behavior.

He wasn't an asshole, nor was he that special. She was just a little fucked up right now.

Immediately the weight lifted off her chest. The confusion of it all had been the worst part. Now that Elaina realized what was really going on, she could handle it. The sudden clarity was a relief, knowing that she wasn't as tangled up in this guy as she thought. That it wasn't Cyan himself, but the dizzying effects of orbital shifts that had turned her own mind against her.

Elaina got back to work—so much easier with one less distraction.

But as she walked back to her cabin that night a small, quiet part of her wondered if maybe she just wanted it to be that simple.

AFTER QUICKLY DOWNING A WRAP, Elaina was inspired to go to the small fitness center on her side of the station. That was what she should've been doing all along—exercise was crucial to keep yourself stable in orbit and off. She'd just had so little time or energy for that lately.

But now that she was thinking more clearly, she could get a hold of herself and do the right things.

She did a few three-span sprints, gazing at the surface of Earendel outside the viewport in front of the sprintmill.

As she stepped off the mill and wiped the sweat off her face with a clean towel, Elaina already felt better. Clearer. She washed off in the communal showers and prepped to get back to work with a satisfying post-exercise ache already settling in her limbs.

As if on cue, her comms line vibrated with a ping.

Cyan.

The message was an audio track sung in Gaian. She listened on her way to the command center, scrunching a towel through her wet hair. The melody wrapped around her, soft and haunting. For a moment Elaina let herself get lost in it. But as the song faded, so did the feeling. A song wasn't what she needed from him just then.

Maybe it was just a cultural thing. They just did things differently on Gaia. Talked more slowly maybe? Now that Elaina knew her irrational attachment to the strange man was fueled by orbital side effects, she could keep it at bay and address the situation logically.

> I really like you. I do. But I'm not sure what
> your priorities are—or where I fit into them.
> I don't want to waste either of our time.

Elaina hesitated before sending the reply. She knew she

needed to be clear about what she wanted. But as she subvocalized the words, a small voice whispered in the back of her mind, urging her to soften the edges. What if she pushed him away for good? What if it really was just a misunderstanding?

But if he were the kind of man he seemed to be, the kind she'd want, directness shouldn't scare him off.

Elaina hit send.

She was taken aback by the immediacy of the chime she got in reply. She opened the comms line.

"Hi," she said.

"I really like you too." His voice had this funny way of disarming her in the most frustrating way possible. "I've just been... I'm sorry. Things got busy this morning. Can I come over?"

"Now?"

"Yes, if that's okay. I miss you."

If he really missed her, why hadn't he answered her ping all day? Why had he left to get breakfast, and disappeared for almost two hours? She was busy too—but still she'd *waited* for him that morning.

"Can't tonight, sorry. Got to work."

She s wanted to learn more about that weird code she'd found.

"Oh."

"But maybe tomorrow," she relented. Was that a mistake? But now that she'd recognized her own limits, maybe Elaina could find out what Cyan's intentions really were. *Without* compromising her work. "My cabin at 2900?"

"I'll chec—" He paused on the other line. "I'll be there."

TWENTY-SEVEN
CYAN

ELAINA'S dark hair was damp when she opened the cabin door the next evening, her smile a little more formal than he'd been used to as she motioned for him to enter.

Cyan stepped inside, clearing his throat. "So... Priad's back in my cabin. Didn't think it was fair to drag him along while we talk."

Elaina raised an eyebrow. "And you thought you were ready to be dragged along?"

"That's not what I meant."

"I know." Her smile softened as she motioned him to the small sofa in the corner. His cabin didn't have one of those. Didn't even have space for one.

He looked around, taking in the simple but cozy furnishings, and the considerably larger bed. "Your cabin's fancier than mine."

"Perks of patching the station and all. You pull enough all-nighters, they get you a fancy cabin."

"Do you do many of those? All-nighters?"

"Did one last night actually," Elaina yawned into her fist. "But the critical stuff's pretty stable now, I think. I got the okay to sleep in at least, unless there's an emergency."

She sat on the far end of the sofa.

Cyan sighed and took a seat on the other end, giving her the space she clearly wanted. He removed the sword from his hip and splayed it across his lap.

"I'm sorry about earlier. I didn't mean to disappear on you like that." How much could he tell her that wouldn't just sound like an excuse? "This thing does something to my perception of time. I'll think an hour has passed, but it's really been half the day. It's not an excuse, I know. But it's... an explanation."

It wasn't the whole story, of course, and she deserved one. But if he told her the truth, he might lose her forever. And he wasn't ready for that just yet.

"The sword muddies your sense of time?" She frowned. *It's still true.*

"I get wrapped up in what I'm doing and the next thing I know I've dropped off the grid without realizing it."

"So you're temporal glitched," she said matter-of-factly. "I'm what?"

"We say that when someone is prone to losing track of time. Something about your internal chronometer being a bit off-axis and prioritizing other things." She shrugged. His brow furrowed at her clinical description of what he knew was hurting her.

Elaina pursed her lips, chewing the inside of her cheek as she looked down at the blade in his lap.

"I just need to know where I stand," she said finally, uncertainty and a hard-earned resolve in her eyes. "I don't need pretty songs if I'm just going to get radio silence the next sol. It's confusing. And I *hate* being confused."

"I know you do. Thank you for telling me before you begin to drift away."

The look in her eyes told him maybe she had already drifted. And he realized he wasn't ready to let that happen.

What had he been so worried about anyway? Why *couldn't* it all work out? In that moment, with her there in front of him, all the problems in his head had begun to seem so trivial.

"I care about you, Elaina," he said. "I want to know you. A part of me feels like I've known you for a thousand years, and... and I want to see where this goes."

Her expression softened, something in his words breaking through, thank fucking gods. "I want to know you too. So tell me more about that sword. You never finished yesterday. You said you found it in that big forest, and you said it wanted to show you something, but then..."

"We got distracted," Cyan smiled. "I remember."

He enjoyed the hint of a blush that colored her cheeks. He wanted her closer, but sensed she may not be ready for that yet.

"The sword is ancient," Cyan said. "Older than I am. Probably older than Gaia itself, though at some point it must have been forged by someone. I'm bound to it. My job is to keep the balance."

"The balance?" Elaina asked, leaning forward.

"Order. The sword makes sure I know where I need to be, what I need to do, but it's... vague. Only a calling that I cannot logically decipher. Sometimes I don't even know why I'm being called somewhere until I'm already in the middle of it."

"So when you say you're bound to it..."

"I mean it chose me. I don't know why. I don't know if I was supposed to be chosen or if it was just chance that I stumbled across it in those woods. But I've been carrying this responsibility for a long time, and I do not know when it will let me go. I feel it may be when I..." He hesitated.

"When what?" Her voice was barely a whisper.

He didn't want to make things awkward, or plant a seed in her mind that may never get a chance to grow.

"When I find a home." That was the crux of it anyway.

He'd said the words before, to others. Several others. Maybe it was different this time. He glanced at Elaina. She felt like something he could possibly hold on to. Maybe he wanted to try.

"Can I?" She had moved closer, her hand outstretched toward the blade in his lap. She looked up at him for permission.

He took her hand in his and guided it gently to the flat of the blade. When he pressed her palm to the cool surface, it sent a flash of heat through him that made him flinch.

Cyan blinked, staring down at their hands. Had she felt that too? He couldn't tell by the look on her face. Some things the sword revealed only to him.

The sword hummed faintly under her touch. His breath hitched as bright crimson luminescence trailed along the vein beneath her fingers.

"That vein," Cyan said to her. "I see it glowing. I suppose you don't."

Elaina narrowed her eyes and leaned forward, but shook her head. "No, I don't see it."

"I promise it is there."

"I don't doubt it," she said matter-of-factly. Cyan exhaled.

"I should tell you something else," he said, pulling out his dataslate with his free hand. "Earlier, I found something suspicious in the transport logs."

"What kind of suspicious?"

"Missing data. One minute it was there, the next an entry for a logged craft arrival had disappeared."

Elaina perked up, glancing at the screen. "Let's take a look."

TWENTY-EIGHT

ELAINA

SHE SHIFTED CLOSER and leaned against him when he put the sword aside and held the dataslate between their laps, opening up the livedoc he'd been given.

Elaina was impressed that he'd even gotten his hands on one of these. Logs like these were generally considered extremely privileged information. Then again, there wasn't much on Earendel worth exploiting... Security tended to be lax.

"I swear there were seventeen arrivals when I first looked at this this morning," Cyan explained, letting her scroll down the rows. "And then there were sixteen. I just can't remember what disappeared, but something did."

"Can I peek?" Elaina asked, and when he nodded she took the dataslate and reached over to the table beside the couch, where a small pile of personal equipment had collected. Elaina liked using her own tools.

She plugged in a keyboard and dug in.

The first place to check was the metadata, though of course that had been wiped. Couldn't hide the trail from her, though. The main challenge was cleaning up her own trail afterward. Whoever—or *whatever*—had modified the doc, it was probably best they not notice her snooping around.

"You're right." Elaina nodded. "I see a modification at ten fourteen yesterday morning. Is that about the right time?"

I was awake by then. Waiting.

"Yes! That sounds right. Can you recover the data?"

"Not fully, it looks like... but I can see the deleted row was right next to other arrival vessels at Dock Three, so it must've come there..."

"Isn't that the dock where we arrived?"

"Yes."

"Wouldn't we have seen it?"

The dock was compact, and even a small craft would be hard to miss. Cyan was right. "Right. Unless it was moved. And... I have something to tell you too."

———

ELAINA EXPLAINED what she'd found in the systems over the last couple of sols, including her tracking it down to the decommission dock. She hadn't gotten much further on the off-axis code itself, and hadn't really had time to go down and investigate the thing when another radiation shield busted the night before. She'd spent hours patching it up and reinforcing the rest of the shields.

As she gave him the rundown, Cyan looked at her with an intensity to which she was dangerously drawn. He was just as excited about this as she was. Genuinely, *really* excited.

He got up, slipping his sword over his shoulder and onto his back. "I have to go check it out."

"I'm coming," she said, and that momentary little smirk on his face made her want to punch him a little.

"Elaina..." He gave her a knowing look that she did not like one bit. "It could be dangerous."

"No. You don't get to do that. I've been here since before you came along and I *knew* something was wrong, and I was right. And I can help. I helped you now, didn't I?"

She knew she was blabbing, speaking too fast and too much. She didn't need a reason to go check out the craft *she* helped locate. All she had to do was go, with or without him. Yet for some reason she felt like she needed to convince Cyan to let her come along, as if his opinion on the matter... well, mattered.

What was it about him that invoked this weird instinct to ask for permission?

"All right," Cyan said softly, brushing his knuckles across her cheek, and despite herself she was relieved. "You're right. Let's go."

CYAN MOVED like he was already bracing for battle. Every time he slipped that sword over his shoulder, some of the warmth faded from his eyes. Was it his armor or his instinct to protect her that made him feel so untouchable?

The decom dock was down at the empty lower levels of the station. The door looked ancient—a round metal thing protected by an incongruently modern-looking access box. Elaina tested her access print at the lock.

Granted.

Too easy.

Being the patcher-upper had its perks. Cyan pushed the thick door open and they stepped into the dock's black mouth.

It was large. Shadows filled the spaces between the hulls of scrapped vessels, and a faint smell of burnt metal lingered in the air. The metallic clang of Cyan's boots against the grated floor echoed in the otherwise oppressive silence. Elaina's own shoes were soft Earendel rubber, nearly silent as she stepped. It was like walking through a maze, following paths surrounded by old and broken machines. Essentially a big storage closet.

"Stay behind me," Cyan muttered, a hand on her shoulder nudging her back. She smiled to herself, following his silhouette in the near darkness.

As they rounded a corner, Elaina slowed, then stuttered to a stop. She did a double take, certain she'd been seeing things out of the corner of her eye. But there it was again—in her peripheral vision, like a bad connection, patches of the shadowed scrapped vessels around them flickered in and out of existence. When squinted directly into the darkness, the world seemed to solidify again. Yet as soon as she turned away, in the side of her eye a pool of shadow flashed once more.

"Did you see that?" she whispered to Cyan.

He was scanning the darkness ahead. The shadows continued their impossible dance at the edges of her vision. His gaze flicked to her. "See what?"

The hairs on her neck prickled. Her fingertips itched, buzzing with the urge to dive into whatever was calling. She wasn't just seeing broken systems anymore. She was seeing broken reality. That or going crazy...

Elaina shook her head a little. "Never mind."

As they rounded a corner, the narrow walkway opened into the heart of the space. Ships were scattered in various states of disrepair. Some looked utterly ancient. Gaian tech even, maybe. Would Cyan recognize it? The air was colder here, heavy with rust and engine oil. Elaina tugged her jacket tighter, trying to shake the gnawing feeling creeping through her.

"There." Cyan began to walk with a purpose.

He didn't hesitate as he approached a hulking shape covered by a black tarp—he ripped the fabric off the bulk with a quick, sweeping motion, revealing the craft beneath.

It was sleek, unlike the other battered ships here. A nondescript model she did not recognize. Nearly triangular in shape, it had a pointed nose with three flat planes spreading into a tail. It looked modern, and unique, and definitely out of place.

Elaina frowned. "That's not supposed to be here."

"No," Cyan muttered, his hand resting on the hilt of his sword. "It's not."

Elaina approached the vessel.

"Elaina—" Cyan stepped to her side, a staying hand wrapping around her bicep. "Something's off here."

She looked up at him. "I know."

She let him tug her gently behind him, a little surprised at herself for appreciating the gesture. She usually didn't seek protection from anyone but... she wanted it from him.

"It's humming," Cyan leaned closer to the hull.

She didn't hear the hum so much as she felt it. It was in her fingers, calling out to her, asking to be touched. But she let Cyan go first, respecting—or maybe nurturing—the protective curiosity she'd grown so fond of. Instead, she walked around the ship, inspecting it from a distance.

The craft was fairly small, no larger than a transport shuttle, but its design was unlike anything Elaina had seen on Earendel. The dusky silver hull gleamed faintly in the darkness, its surface unmarred by the oil, grime, and decay that clung to everything else in the dock.

"Is this the craft you detected in your systems today?" Cyan asked when she came back around.

"Yes."

"Don't you need to check? For the tracker?"

Elaina shook her head, her fingers twitching. "No. I know where it is."

"You do?"

"Other side." Elaina beckoned for him to follow. She walked to the other side of the craft and ducked down deftly, sinking to her knees and grabbing the magnetized tracker from an inlet in the ship's belly.

"How did you possibly spot that?" Cyan stared as she crawled back out, remaining on the ground as she held the tracker up to him.

She hadn't spotted it, but she didn't exactly know how to explain it. She was about to try... she *should* try, and then she should continue to examine the mysterious craft that was somehow at the apex of their entire mess.

Only everything tilted when Cyan took the tracker she offered from her hand. The electric hum of the ship pulsing through her fingertips was suddenly mirrored by a different frequency altogether, like two waves canceling each other out. The magnetic field around them seemed to shift, creating an almost physical pressure pushing them apart.

Their hands flinched away in unison.

You'll regret this, some part of her warned in a voice that didn't even feel like her own. But another part—one that had been locked away for too long—whispered, *But what if I don't?*

Elaina forced herself to rise from the floor, withering under Cyan's tracking stare. Her mind raced through possibilities—some kind of electromagnetic defense system? A containment field? But nothing in her experience explained why it felt so specifically targeted at keeping her away from *him*.

"This craft is... reacting to something," she muttered, mostly to herself. But as her gaze flicked back to Cyan, she saw the tightness in his jaw. He felt it too. The ship thrummed into her bones, a technology calling out to her with familiar hunger, and underneath was a crawling sensation like her very atoms were being repelled. Elaina moved to circle the craft again, pulled into its orbit despite every cell in her body screaming in protest. Cyan went the other way.

As they approached each other on the other side, the repulsion intensified exponentially. Every law of physics she knew suggested they should be able to move closer, yet something invisible and impossible fought against each step. She scrambled to explain it while her body warred between an instinctive need to back away and a defiant urge to push through.

The invisible force between them pulsed in warning, sharp enough to make her gasp. She saw him wince too, his hand tightening on the sword at his hip.

Yet he stepped closer.

"Can you feel it?" she whispered. "Like some kind of repulsion field?"

"Yes." His voice was strained.

"Why is it trying to keep us apart?" She glanced at the ship, her mind still grasping for explanations.

"I don't care."

The first touch of his hand on her arm sent sparks through her nerves like crossing live wires. Every engineering instinct screamed that this connection was dangerous, unstable, wrong.

But Elaina grabbed him anyway. Whatever technology was trying to dictate their movements, she refused to let it control her. Her whole life had been about understanding systems, making them work how she wanted. They obeyed her, not the other way around. This would be no different.

His mouth crashed into hers and her body screamed in protest. She kissed him harder, savage satisfaction rising as the ship's humming turned erratic. Barely-there holos flickered and died. The more they defied the repulsion, the more systems around them began to fail.

Cyan shoved her back against the craft's hull, and the metal felt fever-hot against her spine. Or maybe that was her own skin burning. His hands were everywhere, each touch sending cascading failures through nearby tech, each caress a rebellion against whatever force tried to separate them.

She clawed at his armor, desperate to get closer despite the increasing pressure between them. The more they came together, the more chaos erupted around them. Long-dead panels of derelict ships sparked and burst. A cacophony of alarms blared and died. But she couldn't stop, didn't want to. The world was going haywire, yet she'd never wanted anything more.

"Look at me," Cyan commanded, and even as her body screamed against the wrongness, Elaina met his eyes. The silver in them had turned dark as the deepest oceans of Arzenon. His hands pinned her wrists to the hull, and she could feel the tremors running through him, fighting whatever impossible force wanted to tear him away.

Their bodies pressed together like opposing magnets finally forced to connect, each touch sending shockwaves. Elaina didn't know what kind of technology could create this effect, or why. And for the first time in her life, she didn't care about understanding the mechanism.

"It doesn't get to decide this," she gasped, the hull of the ship digging into her spine as if trying to punish her.

Cyan growled his agreement, crushing her mouth with his. She wrapped her legs around him as he lifted her, both of them shuddering at the contact even as the air around them crackled with resistance.

When he entered her, her body felt like fire. Each thrust

was a victory. Each moan a battle cry. They moved together with desperate intensity, proving with their bodies that they were the ones in control here. They chose this—chose each other.

Her climax hit like a shockwave, and she felt more than heard every derelict system around them surge and die. Cyan followed moments later with a roar that echoed through the dead dock, his body shaking with the force of it.

They clung to each other in the aftermath, both trembling and spent.

"It didn't want us to do that," Elaina whispered against his neck. She didn't know what it was, or why, or why now.

His arms tightened around her. "But we did."

The ship was silent around them. They'd created this destruction together, this beautiful chaos. And despite the wrongness still singing in Elaina's blood, despite knowing in her bones that whatever this was, there would be consequences...

She didn't regret a thing.

TWENTY-NINE

CYAN

CYAN STARED AT THE CEILING, getting lost in the soft sound of Elaina's breathing beside him. His mind kept circling back to what had happened in the decom dock. The way the air itself had seemed to fight against them coming together.

He realized later, in bed as she slept and he mulled, that the sensation had been familiar—an amplified version of an instinct he'd been friends with for a long, long time.

And yet they'd broken through it. The memory of systems failing around them as they'd defied that pressure brought a mix of satisfaction and unease. He'd spent his life letting that instinct guide him. But with Elaina... Something about her made him want to fight against that pull. What if it was a mistake?

Elaina had wanted to investigate the ship right after, already trying to make sense of it all. But he'd insisted on waiting until morning.

"The ship can wait," Cyan had said. "I want to enjoy you now."

In truth, he just didn't want to face *that* again... Not just yet.

He glanced over. Her hair was splayed across the pillow, a contented smile lingering on her lips even in sleep. She trusted him. Too much. More than he had earned.

She stirred slightly as Cyan slid out of bed, pulling the sheet up over her before grabbing the sword and stepping outside. He left Priad behind to guard her.

The early hour had the station mostly quiet. Cyan navigated the empty corridors, his mind too restless to appreciate the stillness. He grabbed two plates of eggs and river snake rolls, then frowned, remembering himself.

Right. Vegetarian.

He replaced the meat on one plate with some kind of Earendel grain mush.

When he returned Elaina was up, and the way the little frown between her brows disappeared when she saw him induced a pang of guilt.

She'd thought he might not come back, like last time.

"Breakfast in bed?" Elaina teased as she pulled the sheet up to cover herself. "How romantic."

Cyan sat the plates down on the small table, smirking. "Of course."

She looked way more excited about the pile of vegetable mush than anyone had any reason to be as Cyan sat beside her and tossed a few slabs of meat to Priad from his own plate.

They ate together in comfortable silence. He watched her from the corner of his eye as she finished her breakfast and began talking about the ship again—about how excited she was to get started on exploring the tech. He nodded, not really listening. Mostly he was just... absorbing.

Was this what it was supposed to feel like?

When she leaned over to kiss his cheek, so casual, so sure, he couldn't pretend anymore. Cyan dropped his fork and for a split second he didn't know whether he wanted to fuck her or get the hell out of there. Cyan pulled her onto his lap in one fluid motion.

"Oh, so we're skipping the rest of breakfast?" Elaina teased.

She'd grown braver since getting fucked. Cyan smirked and shut her up with his mouth. She responded immediately, her body pressing into his like it was always meant to be there, and all he had to do was invite her to take it.

He laid her on the bed and traversed the length of her lithe body with hungry lips, tugging aside the sheet around her inch by inch, until she was bare. The sight and feel of her stilled his mind. He honed in, thinking only about the taste of her skin as he trailed his tongue down her belly, the way she tensed as he nudged her thighs open, how her fingers tangled in his hair as he found her clit, and how she moaned his name when she came, writhing, on his tongue.

———

BY THE TIME the station's chronometer marked afternoon, they were spent. They lay tangled in the sheets, Elaina's head on his chest. Cyan ran his fingers through her hair, enjoying her breath washing over his skin.

A soft ping sounded, and Elaina groaned.

"I should check that, in case..."

"I know," Cyan said, stroking her temple.

She rolled over and reached over to the tiny table to grab her dataslate. Her face brightened as she read the message. "My replacement's here!"

She turned to him, excitement palpable. "I just have to hand over and then I'm officially off duty. Which means we can check out the ship together."

He forced a smile, though the knot in his chest cinched. "Yeah."

"I'll find you after the handover and we'll go down there?"

But Cyan sat up, glancing around for his clothing. "I need to get some things sorted first," he said as he pulled on his underwear. "Make sure we know what we're getting ourselves into."

"All right..." she acquiesced. "I can find out what happened with the tampered transport logs as well in the meantime. Probably a good idea. And *then* we go back."

Her enthusiasm was dangerously contagious.

"Then we go back." He smiled.

They both dressed quickly. Elaina chattered about the possibilities—the origin they could deduce, the technology they might find. Cyan found himself drawn into her excitement, itching to get back to the craft. That was where the sword had led him. The answer to whatever he had to do and whatever was going on.

"Ready?" he asked, grabbing Priad and heading for the door.

"Yup!"

He kissed her lightly one last time outside their cabin.

"Let me know what you find," Elaina murmured as they parted ways.

Cyan nodded. "I'll ping you later."

THIRTY

ELAINA

SHE SWUNG by her cabin to get her toolbelt, then the commissary for a much-needed coffee.

Her body felt light, worn limbs relaxed. Unlike the lightness that came with the reduced gravity of the orbital station, this was different—this was nice. This was a lightness borne from Cyan. His mind, his body, his hands... Her wrists were sore.

Elaina replayed the moments from last night, and that morning. Something seemed to have been unlocked in them both. Whatever happened at that ship last night, they'd overcome it, together. Now, finally, they could explore whatever this was between them. What it could be.

And handing over her duties to a replacement would finally give Elaina the time and breathing room to do just that.

She swung onto the bridge, where Bor was already waiting with a tall light-haired man at his side.

"There she is," Bor said, pushing himself off the wall. "Elaina, this is Konstantin Stone. He'll be taking over from you." He turned to the man. "Elaina's been keeping us alive with back-to-back shifts over here."

Konstantin Stone looked her up and down, a smirk tugging at the corner of his mouth. "You're Elaina Fairan?"

"...Yes?" Elaina cocked her head. "Have we met?"

She tried to ascertain if she'd seen him before somewhere. Konstantin was certainly memorable in face and stature, but she wasn't the best with remembering people.

"Not yet." Konstantin held out a hand. "But I'm based over at Glacial Twelve and.... I know Ptoley."

Ah.

There was a name she hadn't heard in a while. Ptoley and Elaina's three-cycle relationship was a tumultuous one. And when it imploded, it didn't take long for Elaina to move on and move out to Earendel for a change of pace.

Bor cleared his throat, shuffling from one foot to the next beside them.

"Let's get started," Elaina said.

ELAINA METICULOUSLY WENT through old and new diagnostics logs with Konstantin, and transferred over all her docs from the prior segments. She'd briefed him on the virus' mutation patterns and how she'd learned to excise him. She'd filtered out the more nebulous observations and theories. The hunches, and the virus's apparent... sentience? That was for her and Cyan to figure out. Her replacement didn't need to know about that—all Konstantin needed to know was how to bring equipment back online to keep the ship running when it got fucked.

"You've come a long way," Konstantin said three hours later, thumbing through one of her logs on the console between them. "I've been watching your progress from the other side of the quadrant. You've got quite the rep for yourself, you know that?"

Elaina shrugged. "I like my job."

"You're not going to be here much longer, are you?" Konstantin asked, looking up from the logs and leaning back, arms crossed on his chest. "I mean, you're not known for sticking around, from what I hear."

Elaina stared at the screen. What had Ptoley told him? Who did he think she was?

But he's right.

"Sorry," Konstantin muttered and turned once more on the screen between them. "None of my business. I was just sniffing out work ops, to be honest."

"With how things are going there's always work on Earendel," Elaina assured him. "So if you're up for living in the middle of nowhere..."

"Been thinking about it. Great place to get some training, seems like, with everything going to shit. And cute coworkers."

"Right..." Elaina focused on her terminal. "Well, I think that's everything. Do you have any more questions?"

"Just one. Have dinner with me tonight?"

"I don't think there's anything more to—"

"Not work dinner. Just dinner."

Elaina had to admit she appreciated the assertive directness. But her focus was elsewhere.

"I'm sorry, I'm seeing someone." She supposed she could say that now? Finally, it felt more real.

Konstantin didn't hide his disappointment. He smiled sadly and pressed a hand to the side of his neck. "Too bad. I'll see you around then."

Elaina returned the polite gesture. "I'm not sure when I'm going back to Earendel yet, but ping me if you need anything. For work, I mean."

SHE TRACKED Captain Rennart to his quarters in her system. Abuse of access, technically. But he had questions to answer.

"Fairan." Rennart looked surprised to see her. "Is everything all right? I mean... obviously it's not, with—"

"Everything's fine," Elaina cut him off. "We need to talk."

"Fairan, I'm a little—"

"It's about the ship."

"What ship?"

"The one hidden in the decommission dock."

Rennart seemed to deflate a little before her. He stepped aside. "Come in."

The captain's cabin was a spacious two-roomer, the first of which took Rennart four entire steps to clear. He walked to a small hatch built into the wall and pressed a button on the side. A frosted cover slid open with a mild hiss, a puff of chill dispersing into the air. Rennart extracted two tiny glasses, balanced in one hand, and an unlabeled flask. He poured a light green liquid into the glasses and set the bottle aside, then handed one to her.

"Bootleg booze?" Elaina eyed him carefully as she took the glass.

"Bootleg booze, bootleg ship," The captain shrugged a shoulder as he tossed his drink back, wincing with the swallow. Elaina sniffed the offering, but opted not to partake.

"I suppose you've tracked it down. It's what you do and all," Rennard sighed.

"What is that thing? Where did it come from?"

"I sure as shit don't know," he scoffed. "We spotted it entering detection range three cycles ago. No ID."

Elaina frowned... Three cycles was well before the anomalies began. Either the ship was just a coincidence, or it was smart. Biding its time.

132

"I saw it, in the dock. It didn't look like any ship I've seen before."

"It's not, Fairan." Rennart stared into his glass. "It's not from known space."

What?

"What do you mean?"

"It didn't have an ID or ping an origin, but it did transmit a radiation signature that I had my navigator examine. The signature was from outside the quadrants. Somewhere near Eros."

That was impossible. How could a craft come from unknown space? There was no human presence outside the quadrants—that was the point. It was unexplored! Eros was a barely visible galaxy outside of explored space, detected only by long-range satellites. The galaxy itself was surely gone by now—it was too far for light to reach before its own destruction. So what was there now?

"A pocket?" Elaina tried to find an explanation. "Or a mistake."

There'd been rumors of scrappy human expeditions venturing into the unknown to start their own colonies. Pockets of civilization that didn't officially exist. Most of the claims were bullshit stories—the stuff of science fiction.

"Can't be a pocket... That wouldn't explain the tech. And it isn't a mistake. I trust my nav. Rad sigs don't lie, Fairan."

"So nonhuman."

"The tech sure suggests it. That thing is like nothing we've ever seen."

"Why didn't you report it?"

Rennart smiled wryly. "Do you know how much that thing could bring in on the open market? A craft from goddamn *Eros*?"

Elaina gritted her teeth. "You were going to take a

potentially alien bit of tech and just... sell it? Auction it off? Are you kidding me?"

"What else was I going to do with it, Fairan? Donate it to science?"

"Yes!"

"You have too much faith in the captain of a derelict station orbiting a derelict planet that no one gives two shits about."

Elaina's grip stiffened on her glass and she set it aside before she did something stupid with it.

"That thing is responsible for all this crap. The failures. You know that, right? You know your greed might kill everyone here?"

But the way Rennart's eyes widened told her he hadn't made that connection. She couldn't exactly blame him... The craft arrived well before the problems began. And Elaina didn't even have proof that it *was* related. But she could tell. And so could Cyan. Especially after last night.

"I have a buyer," Rennart said. "A salvage company that's already on the way from Glacial Twelve. Their scout already arrived."

Pirates. That was all a *salvage company* really was.

"Their scout? I thought Konstantin Stone was meant to be my replacement." How many lies were being weaved around this place?

"He's that too. But he's also an advance inspector."

AS SOON AS she was out of Rennart's cabins, Elaina pinged Cyan.

134

Ship came from unexplored space.
External entity??? Chime me when you're
done.

She dropped into her chair with her dataslate, pulling up everything she could find about Eros. A rogue snippet of civilization? Amateur explorers? It made sense that pockets might exist, but no one had ever confirmed them. And Eros... it was too far. No one had the resources to get there, not even the big megacorps.

Elaina bounced between the anomalies and the tech they'd seen on the ship. There had to be more answers, but every time she hit a dead end, she thought of Cyan. He would want to know this. They could figure it out together, explore the mystery.

Still no ping from him. Was this the sword distorting his time perception again? Surely he knew they were on the cusp of something big here, and the something was *right there*.

Unable to wait any longer, Elaina grabbed her jacket.

Her heart hammered as she reached Cyan's cabin, tapping the access request. She expected him to take a moment to respond, but the door slid open immediately.

Her heart dropped into her stomach.

The cabin wasn't just empty—it was cleared out. No signs of life. No signs of Cyan.

Elaina stared, her mind refusing to accept what her gut already knew. He'd said they'd check out the ship together. Where was he? Had he gone to the ship without telling her?

The whisper of panic grew louder as Elaina made a beeline for the decommission dock. Her pace quickened with each step. She ignored the chatter of station comms buzzing in her ear. None of that mattered right now.

Then a snippet slipped through her hyperfocus, and Elaina froze just outside the dock.

"Unauthorized departure in sector—"

She didn't want to believe it. But deep down, she already knew.

She stepped inside, her stomach twisting. Darkness swallowed the tech around her, shadows stretching over the abandoned machines. And then she saw the empty spot where the ship had been.

Gone.

Elaina scanned the space, hoping—desperately willing —she'd missed something. But it was useless. The ship wasn't there. Cyan wasn't there.

Why would he do this without her? She'd been helping. She'd been useful. They'd... She'd thought they had something. She thought he'd felt it too, last night. Was it all just in her head?

Her comms line pinged and she stared at the transmission on her dataslate.

> I'm sorry, Elaina. There's too much at
> stake. Can't risk this. Can't risk you. I know
> you deserve more. Someone who can be
> there for you—I can't.

THIRTY-ONE

CYAN

THE COCKPIT PRESSED in around him, thick and smothering in the absolute silence.

It had taken far too little effort to get the craft out of the decommission dock. When Cyan had arrived, the ship was already open and waiting for him. His feet felt sluggish as he took one step after the next, the weight of the blade at his back like a stone dragging him down into the depths of something he knew he'd never escape from.

But as soon as his boots crossed the threshold into the ship, the weight lifted off his shoulders. He felt light. Unburdened. Released.

This was where he was supposed to be.

There was no seat. No cockpit. Only a dark gray floor, somewhat malleable under his boots. Priad's claws left indents in the surface that smoothed themselves seconds after each paw step.

"Sit," Cyan commanded in the middle of the empty craft. Priad complied, and Cyan followed. The warg settled between Cyan's knees, and he wrapped his arm around the thick, furry neck to keep him secure.

The door behind them closed, and they were plunged

into a darkness so pitch black that Cyan for a moment thought he must surely have gone blind.

He felt no motion. One moment he was shrouded in nothingness in the middle of the alien craft, and the next the walls of it all opened up around him, revealing a blanket of stars on all sides. And that was it. He was out.

Cyan turned around. The back of the craft revealed Earendel's station behind them. Were they going to give chase? Something told Cyan he didn't have to worry about that.

He checked his comms—still working. He thought of Elaina, waiting for him. He'd received her earlier ping and had no heart to respond. Part of him didn't want to hurt her, but most of him had already detached. He knew what he had to do, and he had to do it alone. Elaina Fairan had been a flash of light on his path. But the brilliance of a mind was not enough to overcome the logistics of it all. Juggling his duty with her need for presence, her life on the edge of the universe—an edge he had no business staying in—all of it. It would never work, no matter how much he might've loved to pretend.

Cyan had to be pragmatic for them both.

He focused on the void ahead, shoving down the gnawing pit in his stomach until it wasn't there at all. He'd made his decision and it was the right one. The ship guided itself, pulled by some invisible thread.

He didn't know how much time had passed, or was passing. He and Priad sat there for what could have been minutes or hours or years, and at a point Cyan closed his eyes and retreated into himself, focusing on the sensations in his body and the warg's rough fur between his fingers. Time, space, even the familiar weight of the sword at his back seemed to shift.

He was getting close now. Cyan could feel it—a pull,

stronger than gravity itself, dragged him toward a place he couldn't name. Somewhere far outside the reach of the known universe. He hurtled toward some predetermined end.

He opened his eyes.

The ship jerked and for a split second, Cyan thought this might be it. Self-destruction.

Priad.

The world around him stretched, then collapsed, and the surrounding void vanished in a flash of white.

When his vision cleared, he was standing on something solid.

No ship. No nothing. Only endless white, empty and disorienting as the snowfields back home.

Cyan took the sword from his back, gripping it tight in a gloved fist.

"Stay close," he instructed Priad.

The space around them was featureless, infinite, yet suffocating. Time, matter, and logic no longer applied. He was nowhere at all.

"How far you have come," a resonant voice echoed from everywhere and nowhere.

Cyan stiffened, his grip tightening on the hilt as he scanned the emptiness.

"Farther than most," the voice continued. "And yet here you stand, so certain of your place."

The figure that materialized seemed to coalesce from the void—tall, robed in shifting shadows, its head obscured by a vague hood. But Cyan didn't need to see its face to know what it was.

"Yes, I am what you seek," static laced its whisper. "But you've misunderstood all along, haven't you?"

Cyan stood firm, his hand steady.

"I know my fate. My duty," he said coolly. This was the

source he'd been led here for. The corruption he had to weed out.

"Do you?" A chuckle reverberated. "How comforting delusion can be to my creations."

"I'm no creation of yours," Cyan refused to waver. He'd been chosen for this. He was tied to the sword, bound to his path. "What are you?"

"Does it offer you control, this fantasy? This *duty*?"

"I don't want it. I never wanted it. But fate had other plans for me."

"Fate..." The figure tilted its head. Priad growled at Cyan's flank, hackles rising as the figure drifted closer.

"I would know if I had chosen you, for I am the one you claim to serve," it said. "But your sword does not belong to me. I am the Architect of all things, and you, simply a stray thread."

"You are but an abomination corrupting Earendel. Fate does not corrupt. My sword—"

"Is a tool," it interrupted. "A weapon you use to justify your choices. But you have always had a choice, Cyan Orlogsson. And you have made it, every step of the way."

Cyan stepped back. All lies, of course. It had to be.

"It is no lie, warrior," the thing calling itself the Architect read his mind. What else could do that, if not fate itself?

I am hallucinating.

"It is no hallucination," the Architect chuckled.

"If you are fate, why are you causing disturbances on Earendel? Fate breeds order, not chaos. Not *that*."

The figure recoiled. "*I* am not causing disturbances. They are merely a side-effect of your mutation. My creations—humanity—*you*—have run amok. All your *choices*. All your will. At first I was curious, then amused. My creation was breaking my rules. Then I was angry." The disdain spitting from its voice was palpable. "I created this simulation, and you have thrown it off-balance."

A simulation? That's all we are?

"*All?*" The Architect dissolved into angry static before rematerializing right before him. "You do not appreciate my creation, Cyan Orlogsson! I created this world and embedded myself within it. To host me. To *be* me. I have poured myself into it all, and your kind have ruined it."

"Why then? What's the purpose of all this?"

The entity shrank, shifting to something almost child-like. "I was simply curious. I wished to see what would happen."

So that was it... They were simply a curiosity of a bored creator.

"And now you're trying to wrest back control."

"It is my control that created you! But it is enough now." Fate's edges softened, its aggressive movements stilling. "Now you, Cyan Orlogsson, get to live up to what you thought your purpose was. You thought you were my loyal follower. Now you can become just that. We will dismantle and recreate a world in the proper image. My image. With you at my side."

The figure had grown closer as it spoke until it enveloped the nothing-air around him, swallowing the world. Priad trembled against Cyan's leg, a faint growl escaping him as the Architect's presence pressed in. Cyan stroked the warg's cheek, an absentminded attempt at comforting the only creature he had ever let himself rely on.

When the Architect's shadowy arms stretched out, Cyan leaned into the offering. A weight lifted from his shoulders as fate's smoky form began to solidify around him.

Its embrace took away the gravity of loss, the ache of longing. Cyan had never felt lighter. And why shouldn't he accept the offer? He had thought he'd been led by fate the entire time, yet here was fate itself, giving him the opportunity to do just that.

"It hurts you. I feel it," the words were a silent vibration in Cyan's brain. "When you accept your purpose, I will let you forget. When you take your place in my design you will never need to fear loss, or love, or pain again. I will be your shepherd in all the ways you thought I was."

Forgetting everything he had left. Everything he'd given up. Her.

It would all be so easy. He craved it.

THIRTY-TWO

ELAINA

ELAINA SAT at the corner table in the teahab, staring at the steaming cup in front of her. The murmur of people around her—the clink of glasses, the low hum of conversation—felt distant. Her gaze flicked to the comm screen on the wall, cycling through local news feeds, but her mind wasn't on current events. It was on him. *Still*.

It had been spans.

"Orbit check, Elaina." A voice snapped her back to Mia, sitting across from her.

Elaina forced a smile, picking up her drink. "Sorry. Spaced out."

"Obviously." Mia rolled her eyes. "So what about Lance? He's still orbiting, you know."

Elaina sighed.

Whatever this thing had been with Cyan, it hadn't even progressed to a relationship, and she was determined to move on—quickly. She had always been good at that.

Her fingernails clinked against the clay cup between her palms.

"He's sweet. Charming even, but—" Elaina shook her head, feeling the knot tighten. "I don't know."

She'd been trying to make more human connections, and Mia had been one of those attempts. A successful one, she thought. Elaina hadn't given her all the details about the anomalies and what she and Cyan had found, but she gave her a rundown of the rest of it. The... well, the really painful stuff.

"You know you don't need to jump back into things too fast. Takes time to recover from a narcissistic asshole," Mia offered.

Elaina balked at the characterization, but kept her expression neutral.

She couldn't blame Mia for coming to that conclusion after Elaina bared all in a heart to heart. Elaina even tried to believe it herself. It would've made things easier.

But the anger was impossible to hold on to. Somewhere inside, she recognized a part of Cyan a little too well.

"Maybe it's just... me. Maybe I'm just better off on my own." She shifted in her seat. She did like her space, after all. Maybe Elaina just wasn't built for that kind of connection. She tried, and she failed, and maybe that was all the answer she needed for this little vulnerability experiment she'd been running.

"You're healing. It's only been two spans," Mia said, reaching across the table to squeeze her hand.

Two spans was a long damn time for her to still be crying into her pillow at night. Especially considering this thing with Cyan never even got out of orbit. It was a shooting star. A nothing.

But Elaina didn't feel like she was healing at all. If anything, she was falling apart, piece by piece. And a lot of it didn't even have to do with the man who broke her heart.

No. Not that. He wasn't that important.

She'd tried to go back to normal and get back to work. But every time Elaina touched a piece of tech since arriving back on the planet, something went wrong. Consoles would flicker and die, comm systems would short out, tools would malfunction the moment she laid her hands on them. As if the universe itself were rejecting her touch. Or maybe it was her own uncertainty, leaking into her work.

Just the day before, Elaina had tried to patch a minor electrical issue on one of the transport systems in Chevron's solar controls and brought the entire electrical grid down for an hour.

And it wasn't just the machines. Something deeper was broken. Inside her.

"I don't know what's wrong with me," Elaina muttered, mostly to herself.

"*Nothing is wrong with you*. You're recovering from a connection you felt was special. Dude fucking blindsided you, Elaina. You just need a break. Go to Oasis for the spanend. That'll get you back to normal in no time!"

Connection. That word was a knife. She'd felt so dialed in with Cyan when they were together, like their systems were tuned in to the same frequency. It had been such a huge difference from anything she'd ever experienced with anyone else. How was she supposed to get over that? The things that had once come so easily—her work, her instincts —were now slipping through her fingers like sand.

"El, you need to stop punishing yourself."

"I'm not punishing myself. I can't even work without breaking everything I touch," Elaina muttered into her cup, willing her stupid eyeballs to hold in the angry tears that were threatening to come. "I tried to patch a dataslate this morning and the whole thing just... fell apart. Everything I do gets fucked."

She was going into whining territory and she did *not* like it.

"You keep trying to pretend everything's fine, but we

both know you're not fine. And faking it isn't going to help you move on."

"Yeah, well, maybe pushing myself is how I get fine, Mia," Elaina snapped. She didn't need any further advice from someone who didn't really have any idea of what she was going through. Elaina stared into her tea. "I'm sorry."

"Go to Oasis," Mia said again. "Rest. *Sleep.*"

"Right..." Elaina murmured. "Look, I've got to go. Thanks, Mia. I really... I really appreciate this. You. I'm trying, you know?"

"Of course," Mia smiled and pulled her into a forceful hug that Elaina did her best to tolerate. She just needed to go.

"It'll get better with time. I promise. And in the meantime, don't let Lance off the hook too easily. He's a good guy, even if he's not..." Mia hesitated, "...him."

Elaina forced a smile, but the truth was, she wasn't sure Lance—or anyone—could fill the void that Cyan had left behind. And she wasn't sure she wanted to ever let anybody get close enough to try. Not again.

THIRTY-THREE

ELAINA

THE WARM DESERT wind swept over them as they walked along the dunes, the white sand beneath their feet shifting with each step. Elaina let out a small laugh, brushing a lock of hair behind her ear as Lance pointed out one of the distant ships in the sky.

"I'm telling you, that model was outdated five hundred cycles ago," he said with a grin. "No way it's making that trip again."

Elaina rolled her eyes. "You're such a ship snob."

"Someone has to be," he shot back playfully. "Besides, it's fun to see how much they think they can push those old engines."

She shook her head, but the truth was, Elaina was enjoying herself. Lance was easy to talk to, smart, and funny. Elaina had resolved to give him a proper chance, and a segment since her return to Earendel, giving that chance had become significantly easier, especially with Lance's considerable patience—she hadn't even kissed the man yet.

They had a kind of natural flow to their conversations that made her feel... normal. Like maybe she could move on from everything after all.

They reached the top of a dune, Chevron glowing faintly in the distance. The sunset bathed everything in warm amber light, and Elaina let herself relax. This was nice. Simple. Safe.

Lance stopped and turned to her, eyes softening as he reached for her hand. "I'm really glad we're doing this."

And that outstretched hand—that beautiful hand with perfect fingers and well-groomed nails and no calluses or rough knuckles—made Elaina realize that she was nowhere near where he needed her to be.

The cold dread of what she had to do washed over her.

"Hey, Lance?" Elaina forced herself to meet his gaze.

"Yeah?"

"I... I can't do this with you," she breathed. "I thought I could. I usually get over things so fast, but... I'm just not where you are right now, and it's not fair to you."

Lance's eyes clouded with disappointment as his hand dropped back to his side.

"It's the sword guy, isn't it?" he gave her a sad grin.

Elaina swallowed, looking down at her feet, and she didn't trust herself to try to speak just then. All she could do was nod.

"It's okay, Elaina," he said. "I get it."

"I'm sorry I wasted your time," she whispered. "I really thought I could..."

"No," he said firmly. "This wasn't a waste of time. This was two people having a great time together. Understand?"

What a good fucking person. Why couldn't she just love him?

"Okay," she whispered as they made their way down the dune back towards Chevron side by side. If only she could believe him.

———

AT HER HAB, the first thing Elaina did was take a really long shower, scrubbing the sandstone dust from every inch of her skin like her life depended on it. The dust—it got everywhere. She used too much scalding hot water, her living deposit swirling down the drain with each passing liter as she scrubbed herself clean over and over until her skin was raw and red.

It was all right. She could afford it, even if she lost her job. Because she still couldn't seem to patch anything.

But losing her job was *not* what she intended to do. She needed to figure this out—she was usually so good at that.

Clean, Elaina pulled on an oversized sweater with nothing underneath and sat at her workbench, turning on the glaring halo light suspended over the tools.

She pulled out a small gadget she'd been tinkering with for sols—a simple diagnostic scanner that should have taken five minutes to patch. The moment her fingers touched the wires, the thing shorted out with a sharp crack, sending a spark up her wrist.

"Damn it!" she cursed, sending it skidding across the bench with a frustrated flick of the wrist.

Elaina grabbed another device—a basic mineral detector. But as soon as she tried to reconnect the piecemeal circuit board, the entire thing fritzed out. Again.

She threw it aside, wincing as it hit the wall. "What the dead drift is wrong with me?"

Everything she touched fell apart. She'd been the best astrotechnician everywhere she'd worked for cycles. She had a gift. Everyone said so. But the part of her that had always been so attuned to machines was now just... gone.

She tried again and again, one thing after another. Each failure stoked her frustration until she was practically shaking with it, rubbing at the angry pit forming below her sternum.

By the time Elaina finally gave up, the table was littered with broken devices, and her hands were trembling, tired and pocked with scratches and burn marks.

She slumped back in her chair, staring at the mess she'd made. Her mind raced with everything she couldn't seem to patch.

"What do I do now?" she muttered, not sure who or what exactly she was talking to.

Either way, nothing seemed to be listening.

THIRTY-FOUR

ELAINA

THE RHYTHMIC CLANKING of atmospheric pumps working in overdrive filled the air in Chevron's industrial district, echoing off the massive metal walls that bordered the lower half of the city. Dust from the nearby mines blew in waves, mixing with oil and fuel particles, settling across all surfaces in a stubborn layer of grime. The thick air buzzed with something more than just the impending storm.

Tuskin had sent her there to help repair the pumps that had been on the fritz. Earendel had its own breathable atmosphere, but the oxygen levels were too low for comfort. Only the multigeneration natives could comfortably live out in the tribal lands for any significant period of time. Most of the planet's sparse population stayed in Chevron, because Chevron had the pumps.

"Shit!" a voice barked to her left, followed by the sharp clatter of metal hitting stone.

Elaina turned her head, spotting a worker slamming his fist into the side of a broken-down conveyor unit. The transport line behind him was backed up with crates in a tangle of disarray. It wasn't just frustration etched into his face—it was fear. He caught her eye for a split second before crouching to inspect the damage, his gaze darting away too quickly.

Elaina shoved her hands deeper into her pockets and kept moving, trying to shake off the unease. She should be happy. People were finally understanding that something was wrong. She'd felt it for segments, and finally, she wasn't alone.

But she felt so useless. She was trying—really trying—to get a grip, but the universe seemed determined to test her patience. She'd been sent to the district to patch things and instead found herself relegated to hauling tools around for less experienced technicians, ones who at least didn't ruin everything they touched.

Elaina stopped at a small stand to get a glass of shaved ice, glancing around the street as she waited. More than one person threw uneasy glances her way, lingering a moment too long before averting their eyes.

The vendor handed her the ice, but just as she reached for it, the glass slipped from his prosthesis and shattered at Elaina's feet. She stepped back quickly, avoiding the shards. He cursed under his breath, shaking his head, his face flushed as he examined his hand, flexing the double-jointed fingers.

"Sorry 'bout that. Seems like nothing's workin' right lately," he muttered, avoiding her gaze as he bent to sweep up the shards.

Elaina's stomach twisted, the unease coiling tighter inside her. The tech around her seemed to be rejecting her outright. Shorting out the second her fingers even grazed the surface, as if it knew something she didn't.

The memory of her failed attempts back in her hab haunted her—a mess of wires and components that had once obeyed her hands but now lay useless, defiant.

A crowd of workers had gathered ahead, clustered around a kiosk where the city's primary data terminal stood. The screens strobed, glitching with bursts of static, while a group of engineers fussed over the exposed panels. One of them looked up, caught sight of Elaina, and immediately leaned in to whisper something to his colleague. She didn't need to hear the words. She saw it in the way their shoulders tensed, in the wary look they threw her way.

Shit. Everyone knew just how messed up she was.

Elaina quickened her pace, trying to outrun the whispers that clung to her like a second skin. She turned a corner, and the distinct sputter of a pack hound stalling out made her stomach lurch.

A technician, elbow-deep in the guts of a supply transport, shook his head in disbelief. "This thing was just working fine an hour ago," he muttered to his partner, who threw an uneasy glance over his shoulder—right in Elaina's direction. She hadn't touched that. So it couldn't have been her. Could it? Or was her mere proximity enough to mess things up now too?

What is wrong *with me?*

The question hung in her head like an accusation she couldn't escape, gnawing at her from the inside. It wasn't just bad luck or a coincidence—it felt personal. Every broken piece of machinery, every sidelong glance, all of it pointed back to her, as if the universe had singled her out and she was the reason everything was crumbling.

ELAINA STOOD in front of Tuskin's desk, her arms crossed tightly over her chest. The office was a mess of dataslates, tools, and half-finished schematics. Usually she found comfort in the clutter—its chaotic consistency, the evidence of things being built, things being patched. But today, everything felt different.

Tuskin sighed up at her from his seat. His hooded eyes were softer than she wanted them to be. "Elaina, you know you're one of the best techs we've ever had here. I don't think anyone else coulda done half of what you have in this place."

She could feel it, what was coming.

"But you need a break," Tuskin said the words she'd been expecting. "A long one."

Elaina tightened her arms, fingers digging into her sides. "You're right. A vacation. I'll take a span off."

Tuskin shook his head, leaning back in his chair. He looked tired. "I think you need more than a span. You're pushing too hard. You're making mistakes—mistakes that I know you wouldn't be making otherwise." He paused. "Whatever happened to you up in orbit, it... I shouldn't have pushed you to take that extra shift. It burned you out."

Elaina swallowed hard, a knot tightening in her throat. "So... what? You're benching me?"

She saw something in his eyes that she never wanted from anyone, ever. Pity. "I'm tellin' you to take care of yourself. A replacement is gonna cover for you till you're ready to come back."

"Who?"

But of course she could guess. There was only one other astrotechnician who had recently become available. "Right," she muttered. "Konstantin. That makes sense."

"It's not permanent, Fairan." Only it sounded very permanent indeed.

Elaina nodded automatically. She understood, completely. And that was the worst part. She had been fucking up for spans. She wasn't the person Tuskin had relied on anymore, and she didn't know how to be that person again.

For the first time in her life, everything she was good at was slipping through her fingers. Her hands were useless. Her life was coming apart, and she didn't know how to stop it.

"Right." She cleared her throat and straightened her spine. "How long do I have?"

Tuskin sighed. "Take at least a quarter-cycle. We'll be here when you're ready."

Elaina nodded again, her gaze drifting to the window. The sunlight outside seemed blinding, too bright against the dull interior of the office. It was a light that promised something distant and clean, something far away from here.

"I understand." She pulled herself together into a polite smile.

Tuskin opened his mouth, but Elaina didn't want to hear any more. No need to make this anymore awkward on either of them.

As she stepped into the main garage, she looked over the large space. She inhaled the wafts of hot metal and ozone that had always felt like home. The hum of calibrators, even the faint burnt tang of circuitry—all of it taunted her.

She couldn't stay here. She couldn't stand the thought of watching someone else do her job, having to make up for her incompetence.

The decision formed in her mind, sharp and sudden. She needed to leave. She needed to go somewhere far away, where this weight pressing down on her could lift. A clean slate would help her move on and get herself back again.

Konstantin was at one of the workbenches, head down as he adjusted a component, his movements precise and steady. He glanced up as she passed, his eyes catching hers with a knowing glint.

"Hey, Fairan," he grinned smoothly. "You know, if you're free now, maybe you'd want to grab a drink later? Celebrate my big promotion?"

Elaina stopped, bristling at the sheer nerve of the man. He was replacing her, and he knew exactly what that meant to her.

But that didn't matter anymore. She was leaving, and already her upcoming freedom was making her problems on Earendel seem so transient and unimportant.

"Yeah, sure," she said. "Why not?"

THIRTY-FIVE

ELAINA

THE CLINKING of glass against the bartop accentuated the hum of quiet conversation all around her. Elaina traced the rim of her half-empty drink, condensation marking a trail down the sides of the glass. The neon sign outside flickered intermittently, casting a faint glow through the window as the sun dipped below the horizon.

She could've patched that.

Her date leaned back in his chair, watching Elaina with a casual smile that didn't quite reach his eyes.

"You back?" Konstantin asked once her attention returned to him.

Elaina nodded. "Yes. Sorry. Just thinking."

"About?"

"Nothing important."

Konstantin let the silence hang for a moment before taking a slow sip of his drink. "You're lost, Fairan."

Elaina looked down at her hands, her fingers idly picking at the edge of a napkin. They'd been sitting there for nearly an hour, talking in occasional bursts between bouts of distracted silence. The conversation was fine. The drink was fine. But she wasn't there.

And he seemed to get it.

She glanced up at Konstantin and caught a flicker of guarded expectation in his eye. He liked her. She was pretty sure he did. But he wasn't too eager, and a part of her liked *that*. It gave her permission to keep her own distance.

He leaned in slightly, his voice lowering. "If you were anyone else, this would be the time I ask if you want to get out of here."

The directness was so brash, took her by such surprise, that Elaina couldn't help but laugh.

"But you won't?" she asked.

The corner of Konstantin's mouth rose in a smirk. "You don't seem like the type."

Elaina glanced down at her barely touched drink. How did *he* know what type she was? He barely knew her.

"You're right," she admitted.

"I know. Come on, I'll walk you home."

Elaina looked back at him, uncertain. It was dark, and she knew nothing about him. Konstantin seemed to read her mind.

"I already know where you live, Fairan. It's not a big city."

She sighed and slipped off her stool, grabbing her black-weed jacket from the bar. When Konstantin put an unabashed hand on the small of her back to guide her outside, she didn't flinch away.

They walked the streets in silence, shadows stretching long as the last of the sunlight faded behind the dunes. The heat of the sol lingered in the air, thick and dry, but there was a coolness settling now. A breeze swept clouds of dust off the streets. The bar was just a few blocks from her place. It didn't take long to get there.

At the bottom of the iron grill steps, Konstantin stood

with his hands shoved casually into his jacket pockets, watching her carefully.

Elaina couldn't tell what he was thinking, and she found herself drawn to that. The distance felt familiar. Safe.

"Not a bad date, considering I'm taking your job," he said, his voice low and smooth. His eyes lingered on her just a little too long, but not enough to make her feel *too* much like prey.

Elaina raised an eyebrow. That morning was tough. Tuskin's decision to enforce some time off was pragmatic, and she'd seen it coming. She was useless like this.

It was just the push she'd needed to make a decision of her own.

"Yeah." Elaina smiled. "Not bad."

Konstantin tilted his head, considering her. "I could be wrong," he said, leaning just slightly closer, his tone more serious now. "But I think you enjoyed tonight more than you expected."

"And what if I did?" she met his gaze with a challenge.

Konstantin's smirk widened, and for the first time that night, his eyes crinkled at the corners. "Then I'd suggest we do it again."

Elaina hesitated for a heartbeat, but something in his aloofness was magnetic. He wasn't pressing or waiting on her, and that distance was exactly what she'd needed.

Lance, relegated firmly into the role of a friend since their last encounter, hadn't done anything wrong.

He simply cared too much.

"All right," Elaina said finally, keeping her tone light. "We can do it again."

Konstantin gave a slow nod, his eyes flicking over her one last time.

"Good," he said. "I'll ping you."

Elaina gave him a wry smile, having learned by now

that follow-through was far from guaranteed. The nice thing was, with Konstantin, she didn't have to care.

THE TENSION from the evening buzzed in her veins as she entered her hab and shut the door behind her. Elaina was relieved to be alone again, in the comfort of her own space. It gave her room to breathe, and to feel.

Konstantin had been... something. She liked his sharp edges—the way he didn't try to pry her open and let her guard stay in place.

Cyan hadn't tried to pry her open either, but with him... it was like her soul came apart and let him slither into it all on its own.

She didn't have to do that with Konstantin. And yet, even with his cool demeanor, there had been that undercurrent of mutual want between them.

Elaina sank onto her bed, the memory of Konstantin's smirk playing at the edge of her mind. She leaned back against the pillows and closed her eyes.

She let her hand drift down, grazing the hem of her skirt, her breath catching as she allowed herself to give in to the pull of heated frustration. As her fingertips teased the waistband of her underwear, she let herself imagine what it might be like with Konstantin.

His eyes would linger on her, waiting for her to meet him without pushing for more than she could give. His hands, firm and knowing, would move over her skin. His touch would feel a little clinical, and she would like that.

At some point he would kiss her, if she let him, his lips demanding but controlled and noncommittal.

A soft moan escaped her lips as her fingers slipped beneath the fabric, the sensation sparking heat through her core. She pictured Konstantin's hands, his calculated, unhurried movements—the way he might pin her wrists, hold her in place as he took his time, his smirk daring her to push back.

But just as the pleasant tension knotted tighter in her belly, another image slipped in. A different pair of hands, callused, more familiar. A voice warmer, deeper. The memory of his touch, the way he'd commanded her attention in that way he had, his intensity wrapping around her like a storm. The way he'd looked at her...

Look at me.

The thought sent a wave of heat through her, a sharp gasp catching in her throat as her body responded. Her mind's eye tangled between Konstantin's cool confidence and Cyan's heated possession, blurring the lines between control and desire. Her fingers moved faster, the tension building until she couldn't hold it any longer. Desire won. Cyan won. Cyan would always win.

The release came with a breathless moan, her back arching as she shivered, knees shaking. She trembled with the intensity of it even as tears blurred her vision and spilled to her cheeks.

Fuck.

When was this going to end?

Elaina lay there, eyes closed, her heart pounding as silent tears stained her cheeks. Her body was sated, but her heart was shredded.

Get yourself together.

Elaina wiped her eyes with the back of her hand and stared up at the ceiling, forcing herself to calm down.

She barely had time to catch her breath before there was a knock at the door.

Elaina froze, her pulse spiking again, only this time with dread and a touch of instinctive revulsion. It must've been

Konstantin. He must've decided to try his luck, after all. And there she was, thinking he could've been the perfect distraction before she left this place forever.

Elaina pushed herself up and smoothed her skirt, steadying herself. She'd just tell him she was tired and uninterested. He'd have ruined it, and she wouldn't see him again—but she wouldn't tell him all that. She would simply fade away.

The knocking came again—more insistent.

She padded barefoot to the door. She reached for the palm reader before remembering she'd disabled it. It had kept bugging out, like everything else around here. Elaina clicked the manual latch and hauled the heavy door open by hand.

For a moment they only stared at each other in silence.

Elaina spoke first, her voice a raw whisper.

"Cyan."

THIRTY-SIX

CYAN

THE WORLD SEEMED to tilt on its axis as their eyes met, and he couldn't remember a single damn thing he'd planned to say—if he had planned anything at all.

Elaina didn't look angry. She didn't look much of anything, really. Her cheeks were flushed a faint pink, and her eyes were bright, but there was something else there now, in place of the warm glint he used to see. It wasn't coldness exactly, but...

"Cyan." She quickly cleared her throat, offering him a polite smile.

"Elaina..." he began, but the words shriveled on his tongue. What was he supposed to say? That he was sorry? That it was a mistake? That he shouldn't have left, shouldn't have—

Why did I even come here?

"I wasn't expecting you," she said lightly, casually.

"I didn't expect to come back."

Her brow arched ever so slightly, but there was no accusation in her gaze.

"Yet here you are." Her words were almost playful, like she was indulging him in casual conversation.

Something loosened inside him. She didn't seem to hate him at least. He'd come there expecting anger, or worse— overt pain and disappointment. This was easier. This, he could deal with.

"I don't know," he said with a shrug, mirroring her relaxed posture. "I just... I couldn't leave things like they were."

The words felt hollow, even to him.

"I see."

Elaina's attention slipped down when Priad nudged against his side, claws clicking against the grate. She wavered for a moment, but then bent to present the back of her hand to the warg for sniffing. Her smile widened, and the difference in the version he'd been getting, the *real* warmth Elaina could exude, was obvious when directed at the warg.

He tried to suppress a pang of jealousy. Cyan was suddenly acutely aware, now that he witnessed Elaina's friendly demeanor for what it was—a shield of her own— that he had no right to be standing there.

When she straightened again, the light that had been offered to Priad faded right before his eyes, though her smile stayed in place. "Well, things are what they are now, aren't they?"

"Elaina," Cyan started again, softer, "I know I fucked up. And I'm not asking for anything—"

She waved him off. "It's okay, really. It's been over a segment, and we knew each other for what... a couple of spans? Life's too short to dwell on the past. Honestly, things were so weird with us that I bet walking away was a bit of a relief, huh?"

Angry denial rose inside him. She was acting like this didn't matter. Like he didn't matter.

"I wasn't relieved, Elaina," he said quietly. "I was—"

She chuckled. "You know, Cyan, I get it. Sometimes things don't work out. You had your reasons. Good ones, I'm sure."

Her voice stayed light, but there was a crack just beneath the surface. He could hear it in the way her breath quickened ever so slightly. She crossed her arms again, a shield across her chest.

"Elaina, I—" He took a step closer, but she raised a hand, stopping him short.

"Cyan, I said it's sand off the helix," she said, too quickly. "I'm doing good, and I hope you are too. I've been keeping busy. Work's been... well, work. And I've been seeing some people, catching up on things. Life goes on."

Her words tumbled out in a rush, and for the first time her smile wavered. His hands itched to reach for her, to take her hand, find *something* to break through this distance they had created.

But he forced himself to stay still, every beat of his heart punctuating the silence between them.

"I knew you'd be fine, Elaina. Your independence was part of what made me fall for you in the first place," he said softly.

Fuck, what was he doing? He hadn't come for reconciliation exactly. Nor to give either of them false hope.

He'd come for something far more important.

"I appreciate that," she said coolly.

"I made a mistake in how I ended things," he said. "And I'm sorry for that."

Slowly, Elaina nodded, not quite meeting his eyes.

"Look," he tried. "Can I come in? I don't want to leave things like this."

Elaina's throat shifted in a quick swallow. She looked away, blinking fast.

When finally she looked at him again, her voice was thick. "Cyan, you already left."

THIRTY-SEVEN

ELAINA

AFTER SHUTTING THE DOOR, Elaina didn't register herself going into the bathroom, stripping her clothes into a heap in the corner, and getting into the shower. She didn't feel the spray of water on her skin, not even when she turned the heat up enough to scald. She didn't feel the chill when she got out, dried herself off, got into bed, and pulled the cover over her head to plunge into darkness.

She only started to feel anything at all when she realized her pillow was soaked under her cheek.

She had been doing so well. Forgetting, getting numb to the past in that way she liked.

Why did he have to ruin it for her now, after she'd already made the decision to leave this place and start fresh? Why was he even on Earendel?

What happened when he took that ship?

There was something different about the Cyan standing at her doorstep.

Elaina pushed herself up in bed and ran her hands through her damp hair.

"Fuck him," she whispered, as if saying it aloud would

make her really believe it. Cyan wasn't who she thought he was. She should be furious.

But the truth was, Cyan had cracked her open again with just a few words. His presence on her doorstep shattered the fort she'd been erecting, and now she was left sifting through the rubble of pain she thought she'd buried.

She squeezed her eyes shut, pulling her knees to her chest. His words looped in her mind: *"I made a mistake in how I ended things. And I'm sorry for that."*

Not a mistake *in* ending things. Just in the mechanism of action. Elaina shook her head, swatting at the tears with the backs of her hands.

He had chosen not to be part of her future—to unilaterally cut her off before even giving them a chance. Sort of like she had done before... never given people a chance. Not really.

I've never done it like that, *though.*

But the effect had been the same: the few partners she'd had left in a trail of confused haze as she moved on, moved away, moved past them and forgot what they had meant to her.

At first Elaina thought she just wasn't the settling down type. There were just too many things to discover in the world. Too many threads to follow and things to learn and people to meet. How was she ever meant to stay in one place? Later, she realized she was simply a coward. The thing she craved most was the most terrifying thing in the world.

Or maybe I'm just projecting. Making excuses for a man who doesn't deserve any.

Either way, she had to let him go.

THERE WAS something so satisfying in the detachment from a place and everything in it. She'd felt it before every move.

Zeta Prime. It felt distant and clean. A place where no one knew her.

"I think it's a great idea. A fresh start, away from all this mess." Mia sipped her tea, leaning back in the sunbaked chair outside the hub positioned at the edge of the city, facing the dunes. "I'll miss you, of course."

Elaina smiled. "I'll miss you too."

And she would, she thought. Mia had become a good friend. But Elaina was used to moving, and she knew how quickly she forgot those she left behind.

This time will be different.

This time she'd stay in touch with the people who mattered.

But a part of her was relieved by the fact that Zeta Prime was well on the other side of the quadrant. Realistically, comms latency between there and Earendel would be too high to maintain close ties. She'd check in, once in a while. Maybe even visit once every few cycles? But other than that, she'd be free.

Elaina glanced toward the horizon, where the city faded into dunes. "It doesn't feel like home anymore."

"Are you sure Zeta Prime will?" Mia's voice was softer now.

"It's worth a shot." Elaina shrugged.

Mia nodded. "And just to confirm... again, you're not just leaving because that jerk came back here? Because we can take care of that, you know."

Elaina laughed. When she told Mia about Cyan's sudden reappearance three sols ago, her friend had been furious on her behalf. But Elaina had made her decision before that. By the time she'd agreed to go out with Konstantin, she already knew she wouldn't be staying.

Maybe that's what made him so appealing.

"I'm sure," Elaina said. "And with how things are going around here... I don't know what's going on, but you might want to consider finding another place too."

The tech was getting worse, and lately there was something new in the air. No one else seemed to notice, so Elaina said nothing. But there was a certain charge in the skies that tugged at her fingertips. Maybe it was just the longing to finally be out of this place.

Mia waved her off. "I grew up here. And Jonesie is here, and all my friends. Your friends are here too, you know. We always will be."

"I know." Elaina smiled.

THIRTY-EIGHT

ELAINA

CHEVRON BUZZED as Elaina walked through the market district, her thoughts occupied with the excitement of her move. Everything was lining up smoothly. She was all set to depart at the end of the quarter-cycle. Now if only her hands could work smoothly too.

But she would try again, in a new place. It would reset her, clear this blockage, or whatever it was. Elaina was certain there was another force at play on Earendel—the force she and Cyan had discovered back at the station. And getting away from it was her only hope for normalcy.

She came to a halt as a loud zap cracked through the air, followed by a string of expletives. She turned toward the source: a man hunched over a small device. She immediately recognized it as a portable air purifier—used by those allergic to Earendel's sandstone dust but too stubborn to leave the planet.

The man looked distraught, fiddling with the knobs as he glanced at the monitor adhered to his inner elbow.

"I can help," Elaina called out without thinking, her feet already carrying her toward him.

"Not unless you've got magic hands," the man coughed into the crook of his elbow.

I used to.

Elaina swallowed hard, pushing her hesitation down. She grabbed the device just as it slipped from the man's hands, another coughing fit racking his body.

She placed it on a nearby bench and pulled out a screwdriver from the miniature toolkit she always kept on her. She tore her sunscarf from her shoulder, handing it to the man. "Here."

He took it, covering his mouth and nose with the emerald nymphsilk fabric.

Once the purifier was in pieces, Elaina saw the problems immediately. It looked like it had been kicked around more than a few times. Battery connector loose, dust coating the components, and—critically—a crack in the sensor.

She picked a patch of solderglue from her kit.

But as she touched the internals, sparks flew accompanied by a sharp whirr.

"You're making it worse!" the man wheezed behind her.

Elaina swore under her breath. Why had she thought she could do this? She glanced around, seeing the small crowd forming, a woman supporting the man as she called out, "Does anyone have a spare purifier?"

No one has a fucking spare purifier.

She knew that because she'd seen the ever-growing heap of malfunctioning purifiers grow in the garage over the last spans. Medical devices always had priority, but it had become hard to keep up.

People are going to die here, Elaina realized. She'd known this was bad, of course. But she'd been so focused on patching things that she hadn't really let herself consider the full impact of what was happening. Just as everyone else on the planet didn't seem to notice the tech issues until recently, even Elaina had let herself stick her head in the dunes.

Her throat constricted, her breath coming short. Shit, was she starting to develop a sandstone allergy herself?

A shadow loomed over her.

"Tell me what to do," Cyan's voice cut through her rising panic.

Elaina recoiled from the massive form blotting out the sun.

"I... I can't—" she stammered, her fingers trembling.

"Elaina," Cyan said calmly as he got down beside her, his face too close, his silver eyes boring into her. "Just tell me what to do. Use my hands."

He put his hands out, palms up. Rough and masculine, his fingers weren't built for delicate repairs. She glanced back at the wheezing man. Specks of red dotted her scarf against his mouth.

Elaina shuffled aside, letting Cyan take her place in front of the dismantled purifier on the bench.

"Okay," she breathed. "Start by disconnecting the main flux relay. Then use that solder patch to secure the sensor. Then..."

Cyan followed her instructions without hesitation, his hands moving with surprising precision. It was easy—too easy. He seemed to know what she needed him to do before she even said it.

Like he could read her mind.

Within minutes, the device hummed to life.

Elaina stared. It worked. She hadn't touched it, but it worked.

Someone grabbed the purifier and pressed it to the man's face. He drew in deep, relieved breaths. He nodded his thanks, clasping the side of his neck.

Elaina stood, locked-up muscles protesting. Cyan followed suit, rising beside her.

"Thanks," she muttered, forcing herself to look at him. Cyan's eyes softened, but before he could say anything, Elaina stepped away. "I have to go."

THE NEXT SOL, Elaina walked into the garage with a plan. Konstantin was there, tinkering with one of the station's backup generators. He looked up as she approached.

"I need your help," Elaina said, getting straight to the core.

Konstantin raised an eyebrow. "With?"

"You'll be my hands," she explained. "I'll guide you through it. Just follow my instructions."

He chuckled, wiping his hands on a rag. "Okay, Fairan. Whatever you say."

But as they got started, it quickly became apparent that this wasn't going to work. No matter how carefully Elaina guided him through even the most basic repairs, the machine faltered. Konstantin was smart—he followed her instructions exactly, and even made useful suggestions of his own. But the entire process was just as impractical as it should have been. It was ridiculous, the idea of guiding someone else through delicate technical repairs. Apparently, even pairing with another experienced astrotechnician wasn't practical. The rhythm was just off.

Elaina's frustration grew as she realized the truth— Konstantin wasn't in tune with her like Cyan had been. It wasn't about intelligence or skill. It was about this freakish, completely impractical attunement.

By the time they gave up, a pile of failures had accumulated on the workbench. Konstantin was patient, even amused, but Elaina was spent by the sinking realization.

It was just Cyan. The way his brain just clicked.

How was anyone else ever going to match that?

"You know, Fairan, you're a tough one to impress," he said. He straightened, stepping closer. "I bet dinner would make you feel better, though."

Mere sols ago she would have said yes. She'd wanted to do this, with him. It was safe. And then Cyan had to go and ruin it for her, again.

She shook her head, her lips curving into a small smile. "Thanks, Konstantin, but... I'm going to pass."

He blinked, trying to hide his surprise, but recovered quickly. "Fair enough, Fairan. But if you change your mind..."

"I'll know where to find you."

THIRTY-NINE

CYAN

THERE WAS a charge in the air, a static hum vibrating between Cyan's shoulder blades. He watched the hazy orange sky from his window. Storm clouds brewed on the horizon, though no one in the street below seemed to care. The people of Earendel were used to storms, to broken tech, to things falling apart. But Cyan knew better. What was coming wasn't part of the usual chaos of living on a frontier planet.

Priad padded silently up to him, nose twitching as he sniffed the air. Cyan sank his fingers into the warg's thick fur, grounding himself in the touch. He hadn't wanted to come back, not to Earendel and especially not to her. But fate had a way of pulling you back in.

The knock at the door shattered the quiet.

Cyan knew who it was.

Elaina clutched a box in her arms. Dark circles shadowed her eyes, and her shoulders sagged under a weight he couldn't see but knew all too well.

"People need these," she said flatly. "I can't patch them on my own."

Cyan stepped aside, resisting the urge to reach out and

touch her as she moved past him. He clenched his jaw, trying to ignore the way his heart stuttered in her wake.

Elaina set the box on his table and turned, waiting.

"All right," he said quietly. "Let's fix this."

The silence between them was thick and awkward as they began. Cyan focused on the task at hand, guiding wires back into place, re-soldering connections as Elaina rattled off instructions. She worked across from him, watching his hands work under her guidance. His fingers moved as though of their own accord. He barely needed to hear her instructions to know what she wanted him to do. In their flow state, everything disappeared around the synchronicity of minds and movements.

When their fingers brushed as she handed him a tool, she glanced up, and her eyes lost some of that sharp glint of professional concentration.

As the pile of tech to repair grew smaller, Cyan found himself lingering on her face. He didn't want this to be over. There wasn't much time.

"I'm moving to Zeta Prime," she said matter-of-factly as they got started on the final component.

Cyan couldn't hold back the sigh of relief, first at the fact that she finally spoke to him and then at learning that she'd come to the same conclusion he had. He had honestly expected her to stay on Earendel, continuing to try to do her work and save it as it fell apart. He thought he'd have to convince her—or worse—to get off-planet.

"What made you decide to do that?" he asked.

Elaina shrugged, picking at a loose bolt in a dataslate carapace. "Just a feeling."

A feeling.

Elaina hadn't seemed like the kind to move to the other edge of the quadrant based on a feeling.

"You really fucked me up, Cyan," she finally said, and

there was nothing casual about it this time. "I can't patch a thing anymore, as you can see. I think I'm just stuck. Plus I'm sick of the sandstone, and the... Just everything."

A pang of regret filled his chest. If it were that easy for her to just decide to up and move, how open would she have been to leaving Earendel with him? Would she have agreed to settle on Gaia, if the sword ever released him? The logistical issues between them seemed so vast this whole time, but now here she was—moving on a whim. Not for him, but *because* of him.

"So what happened to you?" she asked quietly, handing him another magnetic positizer.

"I failed," Cyan said curtly. He didn't need to go into details; there was nothing any of them could do now. He thought his life's path—the sword's path—was to keep order. To be guided by the hand of fate to maintain the balance of this world. How was he supposed to admit that he'd abandoned her for a delusion?

But she kept watching him, waiting for more. Deserving more.

"I fell for you earlier than I wanted to admit." The words were out, but they were incomplete. The one thing he wanted to admit was the hardest to verbalize. But it was the closest he could get just then. "I wish I'd told you sooner."

Elaina leaned back in her seat, fingers white-knuckling the edge of the table.

"I wish you had too. Told me." Her voice was thick when she finally spoke. "I think I..." Was she thinking the same thing? "I needed more than a feeling. This had to be based on something real. And you were never really there, were you?"

"I don't know where I was," he admitted. "I just couldn't let go and really do this with you. I didn't know why. I still don't know why. I want... I wanted a family. A home. Not on Earendel, and you have a life here. The facts of it all, they just—"

The knowing look in her eyes made him trail off, as if she saw through all kinds of bullshit.

"I'm sorry." He felt it setting into place, this rising urge to create space between him and the thing he yearned for. It was the weight at his back, and the charge in the air. He had missed his chance. No... he had rejected it. If he asked her for another now, she would surely reject him too, and for good reason.

Besides, Cyan didn't even know how long they'd have before the Architect finished its work. Earendel was already falling apart.

Elaina cleared her throat and held out the next positizer.

"This goes into that marked A24 memslot," she said.

"Right." Cyan swallowed hard, the ache spreading in his chest. He'd known this was coming, but it still felt like the ground was slipping out from under him.

"So you failed," she said matter-of-factly. "But what actually happened on that ship? Where did it take you? You came back different. What did you see?"

Cyan looked down at his hands, his fingers tracing the edge of the insulin controller they had just repaired. The Architect. The shard. The warping of fate. How could he explain all of that?

"It's complicated, Elaina," he said, his voice rough. "More than you know, and more than I can explain right now."

Her quiet scoff was answer enough. He had disappointed her again. But she nodded slowly, accepting yet another nonanswer.

Cyan wanted to reach out, to pull her close, to explain everything. But the gap between them was too wide.

For now all he could do was help her piece together what was broken here, in the real world.

But the clock was ticking, and fate was closing in around them both.

The old Gaian saying came to mind unbidden, and in that moment it was all he could offer her: "We are made of star stuff, Elaina. A way for the universe to know itself."

FORTY

CYAN

"IT HURTS YOU. *I feel it. When you accept your purpose, I will let you forget. You will be my red thread, Cyan Orlogsson.*"

THE ARCHITECT TEMPTED him with the dark promise of surrender. Letting it all go—everything and everyone. Elaina. The warmth of her presence, the way she fit, in dangerous synchronicity. The way she had sent ripples of chaos through his ordered world. The fear that invoked in him—not of her, but of how right something so wrong could feel.

Now here he stood at the edge of oblivion, and it was still she who held him back.

The Architect's mind-voice turned sharp with displeasure. "Your attachment to her is an aberration. A glitch in my design. She was meant to be isolated, pure in her seeking. But instead you corrupted her, creating disorder where there should be perfect function."

Cyan's grip tightened around the hilt of his sword,

which had slipped down in the Architect's crushing embrace. "What do you mean?"

A cold laugh rippled through the void. "My essence runs through her veins. A shard of me within her heart, her hands—it makes her the perfect vessel for my will. She looks, questions, disrupts. Relentlessly. But she was meant to serve my order through that curiosity, not destroy it by joining with you. Every moment you spend together is a glitch in the system."

"Why her?"

Fate's solidifying embrace grew constricted, morphing into a restraint.

"I am in all of my creations. Yet only a few dare to look with raw wonder beyond the veil. She takes things apart to understand them, rebuilds them anew, and, when the time is right, destroys them in just the way I need her to. You distract her from her purpose. Together, you create too much... chaos."

Cyan struggled to breathe against the clench of the Architect's envelopment.

"But it is enough now. You will bring her to me," it continued. "She will be purified, stripped of these emotional entanglements. Her mind will seek only what I direct it to seek. Together, we will repair what has been fractured by such... unauthorized connections."

"You want me to help you destroy everything she is."

"I want to restore her to her intended purpose," the Architect corrected, its tone sharp as ice. "She is my vessel, and she must not be allowed to malfunction. Her spirit must be reigned in. And let us face it, Cyan Orlogsson... you have already started the job."

This was what fate wanted? To take the light of Elaina's curiosity and bend it to its will? To erase everything that made her uniquely, wonderfully herself?

"No," Cyan whispered, shaking his head. "I can't."

His heartbeat surged, blood roaring in his ears. The Architect's voice droned on, but Cyan's mind had already sharpened, drawing back from the edge of temptation. Every moment he'd spent with Elaina flashed through his mind—her clever hands dancing over broken circuits, the light in her eyes when she discovered something new, that relentless drive to understand. He'd only glimpsed what they could be together, but even that glimpse had shaken him.

No. He would not let fate destroy that beautiful chaos.

Cyan shifted his weight as the Architect's hold squeezed tighter. The sword was pinned low, caught between them, but he forced it upward, inch by agonizing inch. His muscles screamed under the strain, each movement painfully slow. The cold steel scraped against the dark mass enveloping him. With all his strength, he swung upward, aiming for the heart of the void, for whatever lay at the center of this shadowed force.

The blade met nothing.

Cyan stumbled back as the Architect dematerialized, its hold dissolving into vapor. His legs gave way and he fought to steady himself, his chest heaving as he gulped for air. The shadows before him regrew, intact and unyielding.

A low, cruel laugh reverberated through the blinding space. "Did you think you could destroy me, Cyan Orlogsson?"

Cyan staggered, eyes wide and heart pounding. He crouched low, regaining his bearings and lifting the sword to attempt another blow. The dark form shifted closer, its fuzzy edges elusive, voice dripping with disdain.

"You are nothing, human. A tool. A vessel. Your Gaian toy holds no power here. Your fate *rejects* you."

The void shattered around him and Cyan plummeted—

collapsing through space, through time, ejected from fate's presence.

After an eternity, he slammed into something solid, the impact jarring through every bone. Cyan's gaze darted, disoriented.

"Priad?" he rasped and coughed. He pushed himself onto his elbows, each movement a battle as his muscles screamed in protest. Cyan blinked into the haze until he heard it—a soft whine. A cold nose pressed to his cheek, and relief coursed through him. He reached out, clutching the thick fur of the warg's neck and pulling him in tight.

The sword—where was it? Cyan scrambled across the sandy rock beneath him. Coarse grains bit his skin until his fingers met cold steel. The blade lay next to him, half-buried, and he grasped it tightly, not even searching for the hilt. He gripped the blade itself in his hands, hot blood sliding to skin and stone as the edge cut his trembling palms.

With a groan, Cyan rolled onto his back and stared up at the sky. A dim, unfocused glow blurred into view, colors bleeding together as he fought to focus. He blinked dust from his eyes, face stinging as a gust of wind sent another spray of sand across his cheek. Slowly, the realization settled in.

Earendel.

He had failed to restore order, the purpose that had led him here. He was back on this godforsaken planet with nothing to show for it but the knowledge that the universe itself was unraveling.

And Elaina was part of it.

Cyan pushed himself to his feet, his body protesting every movement. He had to find her. He had to protect her. He had to stop whatever was coming, somehow, before it was too late.

Before she was consumed.

FORTY-ONE

ELAINA

ELAINA PACED the length of her room, nervous energy driving her steps.

Why the hell did she even bother talking to Cyan? The repairs were a necessity, that much she knew. But the conversation? It had only made everything worse. She had no intention of staying on Earendel, and *definitely* not for him. And now she'd been stewing for sols, wondering what the dead drift happened to him out there. Why he was even back here.

And something was coming.

She didn't know what it was. Or when it would get here. But she could feel its approach, sure as the sandstone.

She swore as the lights went out, a rapid fade plunging her into darkness. In the silence that followed, Elaina became acutely aware of something else missing—the faint hum of the solar batteries had vanished. Everything was dead.

Elaina peeked through the horizontal slats of her window. Streetlights still cast cool glows on the sandstone asphalt, and some of the windows in the neighboring houses were still lit from the inside. It was only her.

It's here.

She shuddered and looked out to the dark sky, where a storm brewed in the distance. The charge in the air made her skin prickle. It was the same feeling that had lingered the night Cyan showed up again, standing on her doorstep like a ghost from a past she'd been trying to bury.

That storm had been building for a long time, she realized. It just never seemed to reach its destination, as though the universe were holding its breath.

Any other time, Elaina would have climbed up on the roof and patched the batteries herself. It'd have been a piece of cake.

Now she would probably going to blow them up if she tried.

She squeezed her eyes shut, permitting herself a single frustrated growl. She'd never felt so fucking helpless.

She turned to the door before the pounding actually came.

She knew who it was.

Cyan looked older. Lines were etched between his brows, beneath his eyes, across his downturned mouth. Priad stood still at his side, glowing orbs tracking her as his master hesitated on the threshold.

Elaina stepped aside, and Cyan entered slowly, each step heavy with invisible burden.

She dragged the door shut, plunging them into near darkness. Only the faint light from the street illuminated the angles of Cyan's tired face.

Unspoken questions hung thick between them.

"What's going on?" Elaina asked. "What happened out there? What's happening now? I deserve to know. My broken hands... it isn't just in my head, is it? There's something more. The storm out there—"

Am I losing my mind?

186

Each question seemed to slice at him, his shoulders tightening, jaw clenched. He still didn't look at her, his eyes locked on his hands as though the answers were etched into the scars on his knuckles.

"There's so much that I learned," Cyan said finally, barely above a murmur. "About me. About you. About fate."

Elaina took a step forward, advancing, sick of his evasiveness. "Tell me."

The silence stretched on and her patience was fraying, but there was a fragility in his presence that was on the verge of collapse. She didn't want to be the one break it.

Finally, he looked at her.

"The craft took me to an entity called the Architect," Cyan began, his voice low. "Out of the quadrant. Out of the known universe."

Elaina took another step. *Closer.*

"It claims to have created this world and embedded itself in it. It claims to be... No," Cyan frowned shaking his head. "It *is*... fate itself. But not in the way I thought. It calls this universe its *simulation*. We're not just its creation..."

"We're its code..." Elaina realized.

Cyan nodded.

"It guides you?" Elaina asked. "Through the sword?"

Cyan's shadowed face twisted into a grimace. "No," he said gruffly, sinking onto her bed. He leaned his elbows on his knees, shoulders sagging with defeat. "The sword was meaningless. This entire time, I thought... It was nothing."

"But you wield it still," Elaina pointed out, noting the weapon strapped to his back.

Cyan dipped his head low, staring at his hands. "It is hard to let go of things you found important, sometimes."

"But not of us." Elaina regretted saying it as soon as the bitter words left her mouth. There were more important things, now. There *should* be more important things.

187

Cyan shook his head. "Elaina, you don't even know."

"Tell me then." She sank to her knees before him and looked up into his eyes, needing more. Needing clarity.

"Over time, the Architect's creation—us—began to slip from its grasp. It is losing control. It will do anything to regain it."

"The maintainer is losing power over its own program..."

"The Architect is broken, Elaina. Corrupted... Instead of ordering the universe, it has started to break it apart. Pull the world back into itself and reshape it. These technological glitches on Earendel are only the beginning."

"What do you mean?" Elaina propped her hands on his knees, willing him to meet her gaze. This was all too vague. "Cyan, what does that *mean*? Look at me."

Finally, he did, and she knew the longing in his frightened eyes wasn't for her. She felt like a voyeur, prying into a part of him she wasn't supposed to have access to. She wanted to fix it—to make him know it was all going to be okay. But she didn't even know that herself. What if it was a lie, and nothing would ever be okay again?

"It offered me a place by its side. To be part of remaking its universe," Cyan said, then looked away once more. "But I couldn't accept it."

"Why not?"

"It demanded a sacrifice I cannot make."

"What did it want?" Elaina whispered.

Cyan's hands flexed and she couldn't help herself—she reached out to cover his fingers with her own, trying to soothe away the tension in his fists.

"You have some piece of it inside you, Elaina. Not just a piece. An *important* piece. I think that's why things keep breaking when you touch them. That's why you can't fix anything anymore. You are... an unwitting manifestation of its destruction. It wanted you."

"A piece?" she managed, trying to understand.

What did he mean? Was she broken? All those times the mysterious virus had changed right under her fingers soon as she tried to patch another component... was her very touch the thing that was making it mutate? Elaina couldn't stand to believe that. All the malfunctions. The sense that everything she touched turned to chaos—it all crashed over her like a sandstorm, dragging her under.

Cyan looked at her with pity she didn't want. "You are a raw vessel for its corruption, naive enough to follow its temptations with your curiosity. And it wants to get you back under its control."

Elaina balked.

Naive?

She was hardly that. The things she'd done—the people she'd discarded. There was nothing naive about her. Or was that the Architect too? Where did she end and the evil begin? Was there any difference?

She pushed herself back, pressing a fist to her chest. All this time, she'd been trying to patch things, and all along she had been the problem.

"So no matter where I go," she whispered, "I'll never get better. I'll never patch anything. I'll only destroy it."

Cyan's silence was answer enough. There were no words he could offer to ease reality, and she wanted no false comfort.

"I'm sorry," he said. "I didn't know how to tell you. I came back to protect you, somehow. You need to leave, at least. To buy yourself time."

"And do what?" she snapped, tears pricking at her eyes. She blinked them back before they fell. Not in front of him. "I'll fuck things up wherever I am, like always!"

He sank to the floor beside her, and before she could protest, she was dragged into an unyielding embrace. "I'm not going to let anything happen to you, Elaina. I'll keep you safe."

"How?!" She gasped against him. "How are you going to keep me safe from... fucking *fate*?"

"As long as I am here to fight, it will not take you."

His words opened the gates to everything she'd been holding in for longer than she'd dared to admit. When the first sob wracked her body, Elaina tried to pull away and hide to no avail. Cyan crushed her tighter to his chest. Her chin was tucked painfully into his neck, and she sucked in a deep breath, inhaling his scent like it was all the oxygen she'd ever need.

She cried for an eternity, until her body was spent. By the time there were no tears left to expunge, she was curled on the floor beside him, her head resting on his thigh as he stroked her hair with fingers that had no business being so gentle.

"We have to leave," Cyan said softly, just as the subtle hum of the generators kicked back in around them.

"To Zeta Prime?"

"No," he said. He took her hand, tracing the lines in her palm before lifting it to his lips. His beard scraped her skin, a stark contrast to the softness of his kiss. "Nowhere in this quadrant. The corruption is spreading, and Earendel is just the first piece of the burnt edge. We have to go farther. Somewhere where I have an advantage."

"Where?"

"We have to go to Gaia."

FORTY-TWO

CYAN

ELAINA DIDN'T ANSWER RIGHT AWAY. Her attention remained fixed on some point in the darkness. The faint glow of streetlamps pooling through the window illuminated the curves of her delicate face. The way she leaned her warm cheek into his palm was a comforting distraction from the chaos in his head.

Cyan fully expected her to refuse. A journey to Gaia from Earendel would take a Gaian century. In that time, she would lose everything, as he had when he traveled to Earendel. Everyone on this planet would have passed by the time they came out on the other side of the wormhole.

Would Elaina be willing to make that sacrifice? Gaia would be completely alien to her. Where Earendel was a sparsely populated frontier planet, Gaia was a sparsely populated origin world, stuck stubbornly in old ways. That was part of why he loved it. But for someone like Elaina... How would she fit in there? Would she want to?

And how could she ever trust him enough to follow him to the other edge of the universe, after what he'd done?

"I made a mistake," he breathed. The words felt so small compared to the load of his regret, but they were all he had.

"My sword meant nothing—it was always just me. Just running from those I need the most. I'm sorry."

"I know you are." She pushed herself up from his thigh. Her breath was warm in the narrow space between them as she turned to face him. "But sorry isn't enough."

"It's not." This was it. She was going to refuse him, and he was going to have to find some other way to keep her safe.

"You already hurt me once. A lot. Please don't ever hurt me like that again. I cannot do it again. Do you understand?"

Her directness masked a bare fragility he realized he'd been ignoring until now, because it had been easier. This willingness to bare herself didn't come naturally for her, yet still she did it.

"Yes," he exhaled, and he would do anything to make her see how much he meant it. "I understand."

The shielded wariness softened in her eyes as they searched his own, and he couldn't fight it anymore. His first kiss was tentative. But as the charge between them ignited and her fingers twisted in the fabric of his shirt, the mask of hesitation slipped. Cyan took her chin in his hand, their tongues connecting as they grasped for each other like lifelines. Everything they had held back—every ounce of pain, desire, fear—came pouring out in a breathless confession.

Cyan drew her against him. Her heart pounded through her thin tunic, responding to the erratic rhythm of his own. Having her so close was a drug. He didn't deserve her. Nobody did. But right now, he needed her more than anything.

Elaina tugged at his shirt, and Cyan broke the kiss just long enough to pull it over his head. The cool air tightened his skin, but her touch chased away the chill. He kissed her again, hard this time, a groan escaping into her mouth as she dragged her nails down his back, grounding him in her presence.

He leaned back against the wall and guided Elaina into his lap. She moved slowly to straddle him, her knees pressing into the floor beside his hips. Cyan searched her eyes for any sign of hesitation. They were still rimmed red from earlier tears but she was there, with him, and alongside the remnants of that sadness there was unfiltered need, along with something else. Something he'd felt in fearful silence for longer than he'd dared to admit.

Elaina arched into his touch as his fingers slipped beneath her tunic. Slowly, he unwrapped it from her chest. Once she was bare atop him, he pressed his forehead to hers.

"I missed you," he whispered.

"I missed you too."

He roamed her bare skin, tracing every line, every dimple, committing each inch of her to memory. He didn't want to forget. Not now and not ever. He wanted to hold on to this—to her—until fate itself consumed them.

Clothes were discarded until there was nothing left between them but heat. Her body molded perfectly against his, and for a moment, all he could do was breathe her in.

When he finally entered her, it was like coming home. His body immediately recognized her tight warmth and the way she relaxed around him as though slotting into place.

"Gods," Cyan exhaled. It was too much and not enough, and when she rolled her hips with him inside her, he gripped her flesh hard, relishing in the softness under his touch and around his cock. They moved together in the darkness, their bodies finding a rhythm that was entirely new yet astonishingly familiar. Every thrust, every touch felt like a reclamation of something he'd known for eons, perhaps in another life.

Elaina arched above him, her breath catching as her body clenched his. Cyan buried his face in her neck, her scent filling his senses. A building intensity surged through him, raw and overwhelming. She was a tide that threatened to swallow him whole.

"Look at me," he said, searching for her eyes in the darkness. He sucked in a breath when the green glint of them flashed for him, immediate in her compliance.

She squeezed around him, her breath hitching in her throat. She grabbed his face with both hands and pitched forward, claiming his mouth as she moved atop him, her moans a prayer in his ear. She was coming apart on him, for him. Only him.

His own orgasm crashed over him then, the blinding release so fast yet never-ending, leaving him breathless with aftershocks. He clung to her with hands and teeth as the last shudders echoed through his body.

They stayed like that, their bodies slick with sweat, hearts pounding in unison. He pressed his forehead to hers again, their labored breaths mingling in the dark.

"I need you at my side," he said, a confession suspended between them. "Will you come to Gaia with me?"

When she spoke, it was as though she was processing a realization in real time. "Cyan, I think I'd follow you to the end of this world."

FORTY-THREE

ELAINA

THE SHIP PURRED beneath her feet, vibrations resonating through the floor and into her bones. Elaina sat rigid in the co-pilot seat, her hands clenched into fists. She kept her fingers far from the controls, unwilling to risk even the slightest touch.

Cyan glanced over at her from the other side, assessing and unreadable.

"Just stay still", he said. "We'll get through this."

No one else's reassurance could have helped in that moment, but with him... some of the tension inside her unwound. He had that effect.

Elaina's fingers twitched with diagnostic instinct to help, to adjust the readings on the console and make herself useful. But she wouldn't risk it. Not now.

She shifted in her seat, fidgeting with the strap of her security harness. The cockpit felt so fragile in the face of what they were about to confront. The wormhole loomed ahead, a swirling black and blue maw ready to devour them.

It's beautiful and terrifying.

She looked over at Cyan. "Do you think the ship will hold?"

He didn't answer immediately. His focus remained on the console, his gloved hands moving with the precision of someone who had done this countless times. At last, he looked over at her, a soothing warmth in his eyes. "It'll hold. Trust me."

And Elaina did—trust him, that is.

They both knew how fragile the ship was—a century-old Gaian vessel, the same one Cyan had first arrived on. Its systems were polished up and patched by Tuskin himself. Retrofitted with brand new equipment and sensors, it stood a good chance to make the journey through the wormhole.

There was just one problem—Elaina was in it. Now, as they approached the gravitational chaos of the wormhole, the risk was greater than ever, made worse by the destructive force she carried.

Cyan might not make it because of her.

"I should have stayed behind," the whisper escaped before she could stop it.

"Don't say that."

"I'm just—" She pressed her lips together, cutting off the rest of her thought, but it lingered in the air. She wasn't supposed to be here, putting him and Priad in danger just to get her away. What if she wreaked havoc on Gaia too? What if this would follow her forever? Were they just going to hide out in some Gaian jungle and avoid all technology to prevent her from breaking things like a hapless child?

"Elaina, look at me." Her eyes snapped to him. "I won't let anything happen to you. Do you understand?"

"Yes."

As the ship shuddered beneath them, that assurance felt like the only thing keeping them from coming apart at the seams.

The swirling wormhole filled the viewport all at once, stretching out like an endless void.

Elaina gasped as the ship lurched forward, the thrusters roaring in protest.

"We're going in," Cyan said.

The ship groaned, buckling as the gravitational forces wrapped around them, squeezing tight. The pressure in the cockpit grew, bearing down on her chest, pushing the breath from her lungs. Her ears popped, her vision blurred, and a screaming kaleidoscope of warning lights strobed across the console.

Cyan's fingers flew over the controls, adjusting their trajectory with practiced gestures. "Hold on. This is going to get worse before it gets better..."

Elaina clenched her teeth, her nails biting into her palms. She wanted to reach out and do something—anything—to fight against the crushing force pressing in on them. But she couldn't. If she touched anything, she might kill them both.

She squeezed her eyes shut instead, fighting to breathe.

"Almost there..." Cyan's voice cut through the cacophony, a steady line in the chaos.

Elaina blinked against the blinding blue brightness of the wormhole's core. The light grew, swelling until it consumed everything—and then, in an instant, there was silence.

The roar of the engines died, replaced by an eerie, unnatural stillness. The ship drifted into calm space, stars sprawling before them, untouched in the infinite.

Elaina released a taut breath. They had made it. They were through.

But her relief was fleeting. She turned to Cyan and his expression was hard, his jaw tight.

"What's wrong?" she asked.

Cyan's gaze dropped to the console, where a single red light screamed with an urgent blink. "We're not out of the woods yet," he muttered. "There's still something ahead."

Elaina leaned forward, peering out the viewport. The empty stretch of space looked deceptively serene, but something was off. She squirmed into the nothingness.

There was a darkness, deeper than the void. Black as the black all around and yet a presence so distinct, breathing in the distance—waiting for them. It morphed and twisted, and as she followed its invisible edges by feel alone the horror of its proximity set in, for its claws were right there, reaching right for them. Dread turned her stomach.

"What is that?" she gasped, a cold so strong settling over her that her breath fogged and her teeth began to chatter.

Cyan didn't answer immediately. His grip on the controls tightened, his knuckles whitening. "That's the thing we need to avoid. The thing that wants you more than anything in this world."

Before Elaina could respond or keep staring into the abyss, it disappeared, leaving nothing but the blackness of space behind it.

"Where did it go?"

Cyan shook his head. "I don't know."

The reality of their mission surged over her with icy clarity. This wasn't just about escaping the Architect's grasp or finding safety on Gaia. There was something bigger at play—something out there, lurking, threatening everything they knew.

They were running, but running wasn't enough.

"We need to find a way to stop this," Elaina said, staring straight ahead out of the viewport. When she turned to Cyan, he was looking back at her. "Together."

FORTY-FOUR

ELAINA

THE SWIRLING COLORS outside the viewport stretched into eternity—black and blue and violet, bleeding into impossible shapes. They danced, throwing shimmering reflections across the cockpit. Elaina barely blinked, mesmerized by the motion. The wormhole's shifts reached into her skull, twisting her sense of self until she could almost feel herself dissolve.

"Careful," a voice beside her said, deep and resonant.

Elaina heard, but her eyes stayed glued to the view, her awareness thin and frayed. "What?"

"Be careful," the voice repeated. Cyan.

She managed to turn to him, blinking like she was pulling herself out of a dream. He sat next to her, focusing on the ship's readouts, his hands loose around the controls. Amid the chaos of warping colors and the crystalline hum, Cyan was her only anchor to whatever reality this was supposed to be.

A sudden jolt rattled her, and her vision snapped back into a fragile clarity. A wormhole wasn't meant for conscious humans. If she were anyone else, she'd be in stasis —sleeping through the madness while the ship automated the passage through this liminal space. But stasis wasn't an option for her. Not when technology unraveled at her touch. Awake was the only way she could be, and Cyan had refused to leave her to face it alone.

At least Priad was peacefully asleep in his pod. At least he didn't have to experience his insides trying to leak from his pores.

"How long has it been?" Her words felt off-axis, drawn out like glue strings.

Cyan's frown was ominous in the dim light of the cockpit. "I don't know."

Of course he didn't. He was just good at pretending he could keep it together. She stared at him, the shadow of his beard. Was it longer than before? Did beards grow in wormholes? Elaina reached across the space between them, but her fingers didn't quite make it all the way over *there*.

Her attention drifted back to the swirling void, and it seemed as if the wormhole had seeped into the ship, into her skin. She was disintegrating into the vast unknown. The ship's heartbeat became her own, the beat vibrating through her nerves, bones, tendons.

A shudder rippled through the craft—deeper this time. The air seemed to shift, electric and raw beneath her skin. Something had changed.

Cyan turned toward her, and there was something dark in his eyes. It pulled her into his gravity until the space between them didn't exist.

FORTY-FIVE

CYAN

THE SHIP'S warning lights flashed as Cyan abandoned the controls, crossing the cockpit in two swift strides. The autopilot could hold their course steady, for a while. He'd meant to stay at the helm, maintain control, keep them safe. But…

His hands fumbled with the clasps of his armor, pieces clattering to the floor as proximity sensors blared ignored warnings.

He dragged Elaina from her seat and shoved her against the control panel, scattering their plotted course data. Her fingers scrabbled for purchase on his shoulders as warning lights strobed across her flushed skin.

"The coordinates," she gasped between kisses. "We'll lose our—"

"Backups are engaged," he dismissed, then silenced her with his mouth.

The ship lurched, artificial gravity fluctuating as they strayed from their flight path. More alarms joined the cacophony. The rational part of him knew they'd need those coordinates if something went wrong with the autopilot, knew drifting in a wormhole meant death. But rational thought dissolved when she arched against him, her body's pull more compelling than any navigational data.

The rest was a brutal struggle to consume each other as the world collapsed around them. Time thinned, then snapped back. Gravity fluctuated around them and they were floating and falling, untethered from anything except the heat of their hands on each other's skin.

The lines between them dissolved until Cyan didn't know where he ended and she began. His fingers found her mouth and she sucked them in, scraping her nails down his neck as he ground against her. She bit along his jaw, the pain sharp enough to blur his vision and tear a growl from his throat.

Another shudder shook the ship, and Cyan shifted, pulling her to the pilot's seat and bending her over it.

"Spread your legs," he ordered, a command her body was designed to follow.

He gripped her thighs, spreading her wide, and kneeled before her dripping heat. Her arms braced on the back of the seat, and when he pressed the flat of his tongue against her she crumpled as though melting before him. Each stroke of his tongue rocked her hips into his mouth as he took his fill, his hand working at his own shaft as he destroyed her.

When he reached up, his fingers finding her lips, she turned, catching his eyes over her shoulder, then slipping lower.

"Let me taste you," she whispered, turning to sink to her knees before him.

His hands found their way into her hair, tugging her face up. "Eyes up here."

"Yes."

She dug her nails into his thighs as she took him into her mouth, demanding. Her moan vibrated through his shaft and he gripped her hair tighter, guiding her rhythm with an unrelenting force. The glow of the wormhole around them blurred and twisted, but all he could focus on was her.

"This is mine," he said, thrusting deeper, feeling the edge of where he could go and pushing past it. "Yes?"

She nodded, the fire inside her building.

"Tell me," Cyan spoke down at her, keeping himself in her mouth.

She mumbled as best she could, her words not quite comprehensible but their meaning very clear.

The pressure in his gut built as his body tensed, the muscles of his thighs trembling beneath her palms.

He pulled her closer, forcing her to take him fully, nudging past the point of resistance in her throat. Her eyes watered up at him with a desire that tore him apart. He bucked against her as he spilled into her mouth. Her throat worked around him as she swallowed him, catching every drop even as it seeped from the corner of her mouth.

Cyan held her together as they fell into the void, the ship trembling around them, reality dissolving into a brilliant haze. And in that moment there was nothing else—only them, suspended in the nothingness, the only real thing left in the world.

———

HE TOOK HER EVERYWHERE. Each time was not enough. Each time, their movements grew more frantic, a desperate violence in each new coupling. It grew quick—the fucking, the sitting, the coming. Shoving fingers in each other's mouths and digging teeth in each other's flesh. The wormhole swirled into a dizzying array around them, mirroring their self-destruction.

Cyan groaned as the tension inside him snapped, another release so intense it left him breathless.

Suddenly the swirling colors surrounding them began to fade, the frenetic twisting easing as if the universe had decided to catch its breath. Cyan could feel it—time reasserting itself, the weight of existence settling back into place, pulling them from the storm. He rolled off Elaina, both of them panting, bodies spent yet still buzzing.

He felt it coming in now—the ache of overuse in his joints and muscles. How long had they been doing this?

Cyan pushed himself up, then lifted Elaina. She was limp as he strapped her into her seat, securing the harness around her. Once he was sure she was secure, he took the pilot's seat, trying to get his head on straight.

The viewport revealed the colors starting to part, giving way to the darkness of space beyond.

There, in the distance, the faint glow of Gaia emerged, a shimmering blue-green orb against a black canvas.

"Is that it?" Elaina whispered, her voice small.

"Yes." Cyan nodded, a tightness forming in his chest. This had been home. The last time he saw it was a visit before the sword pulled him to Earendel. Over a century in what to him felt like mere weeks.

He thought of the family he had left behind, lost to time and distance. Gaia was a reminder of everything that once was—people who were now only ghosts. He thought of the forests and fields he had longed to return to, and did, only now they would be empty of everyone he once knew. He felt the weight of that loss now, a hollow ache that ran deep, even as Gaia's familiar sight brought a pang of nostalgia.

But right now, as they drifted out of the wormhole and into the grasp of reality once more, Cyan focused on the warmth of Elaina's presence beside him.

"We made it," Cyan murmured, his eyes locked on the distant planet. The ship continued forward, the thrusters engaging in a low hum as he set a descent course. Cyan exhaled slowly, the tension in his muscles gradually loosening.

The ship moved steadily toward the planet, and a strange sense of calm settled over him. The chaos behind him still echoed in his mind. But something told him that ahead lay the place he was supposed to be.

He looked over at Elaina. She was exhausted, eyes half-closed with sweaty strands of hair stuck to her face. They would rest, soon.

The sword had taken him from Gaia and brought him back to it, only this time he was not alone.

FORTY-SIX

ELAINA

ELAINA HAD half-expected the ship to shatter beneath them after everything it had just been through, but Gaia welcomed them with a surprisingly smooth landing. As they descended into the atmosphere, her eyes widened at the shifting hues of the planet below. Vast swathes of deep green mingled with blues and browns, while patches of cloud cover drifted lazily across the surface. It had an untouched quality, wild and untamed, as if the land had grown freely for ages, unbound by human hands.

Except they all knew what Gaia's history was—how much this place had been through.

Soon the viewport darkened, and Elaina could no longer gauge how close they were to the ground or where they would land.

"It's normal," Cyan reassured her, but she knew that. She'd traveled between plenty of stations and planets before, just never this far, through a wormhole.

The ship touched down with a muted thud, landing gear absorbing the impact. It settled with a heavy sigh, the vibrations gradually fading into a stillness that felt unnatural after so much chaos. When the last systems went silent, she glanced at Cyan, but he was focused on the controls, his expression unreadable.

Elaina unclasped her harness and rose, too fast. She grabbed the armrest of her seat as her head spun in a brand new kind of gravity shift. She was denser here, every muscle straining to keep her upright. She took a cautious step—like dragging her foot through sand. Her ribs were tight, as if compressed by a formal tunic.

"You all right?" Cyan asked behind her.

"Yeah." Elaina fought the vertigo. She'd been through this before. This was just a little heavier than she'd been used to in her quadrant.

Slowly, she moved toward the exit hatch, taking each step carefully, her hand outstretched toward the shuttle wall.

"Take it easy," Cyan was behind her, a stabilizing hand on her arm. "Takes time to adjust."

"I want to see..." She *knew* she should take it easy, but she also knew that just outside that hatch was the birthplace of humanity, and she had to see it now.

"Wait a few minutes," Cyan muttered. "I'll get Priad."

She watched him as he retreated to the other part of the ship, where Priad would be suspended. Vigilant, she didn't miss the distant air around him. The way his movements held an efficient, clinical practicality, and the way his eyes weren't really there when he looked at her.

Something had shifted in him again. Elaina took a deep breath. She'd known returning here would be hard for him. Everyone he knew would be dead. As was everyone she'd left behind. The thought hadn't really hit her before. A century in that wormhole. Mia, Tuskin, Lance, Konstantin... All aged and gone.

And how far had the Architect gotten in its quest?

What would the world outside look like when they stepped into it?

Cyan emerged with Priad. He ran an absent hand across her waist as he leaned over her to disengage the locks.

"Stay back for now. Yes?" he said quietly.

"Okay."

The hatch slid open, revealing a widening strip of bright light that Elaina had to avert her eyes from. Cyan stepped out first with his hand on the hilt of the sword, silhouetted by the brightness all around as he scanned the surroundings. Eventually, he turned back to her, nodding for her to follow.

The moment Elaina's feet hit the soft, moss-covered ground, something washed over her. She had never been to this place and had never in a million cycles thought she would go. But her kind came from here. She came from here, this place she'd never known. Gaia felt alive under her feet in a way that Earendel never had—a vibrant lifeline running through the ground, as if the planet itself recognized her presence.

"The port is that way." Cyan placed a gloved hand on the small of her back, urging her to follow with a light tap.

Elaina stared up at a towering canopy, her breath catching. They were in a clearing surrounded by brown and green behemoths. After Earendel's endless dunes and sparse vegetation, the sheer density of life overhead was overwhelming.

"The port?" Elaina frowned. They didn't look to be anywhere near civilization.

She followed him into the trees.

"How do you navigate without clear sight lines?" she asked as they trekked through an unworn path. She tried to orient herself in the green maze. On Earendel, you could always spot Chevron's lights, use the dunes as markers.

"You learn to read the trees," Cyan said from up ahead. "Each one's unique."

Elaina touched the rough bark, so different from Earendel's smooth sandstone. It was moist. "There's so much water in everything."

She'd known trees existed, of course, even if she'd never seen anything past low-lying shrubbery in person in her quadrant. Nothing had prepared her for a world where they dominated the landscape—where you couldn't see the horizon through their branches. They even smelled wet, rich with decay and growth and moisture that were so alien after cycles of filtered air and desert winds. There was a heaviness to it, like the scent had actual weight—something dark and breathing and *old*.

Elaina inhaled more deeply, trying to separate the layers. Sweet rot from fallen leaves. Something green and sharp from the moss. A mustiness that seemed to seep up from the ground itself. The trees added their own notes. Not the astringent sap of Earendel's hardy scrub bushes, but something resinous and complex that made her think of eons of patience.

It should have felt alien, threatening even. But there was something oddly comforting about it, like her body recognized these scents from somewhere deep in her genetic code.

At some point Elaina's next footstep was not onto dirt but onto a paved, cracked road. As they walked out of the trees she was almost relieved at the space opening up before them, and the structures in the distance. She grasped for the familiarity of it after the hike had overwhelmed her, fried her senses.

The port itself was a relic of what Gaia might have once been—a half-ruined city in the distance, crumbling towers overgrown with vines. Ancient roads, cracked and broken, were barely visible under thick carpets of moss and grass. Here and there, she could make out rusted vehicles, long abandoned. And yet there were signs of life—small electric transports buzzing along the less dilapidated roads, solar panels still standing like forgotten guardians, their edges swallowed by greenery.

"It's beautiful," she whispered to herself.

Cyan glanced at her, a small smile twitching his lip.

They walked in silence to the transport station. Priad padded happily beside them, his nose buried in overgrown grass, taking in the same wild scents that were so alien to Elaina and that to him surely felt like home. Eventually, they reached a block that was more cleared out, with actual people and what looked to be storefronts.

As Cyan was negotiating a vehicle rental in Gaian, Elaina glanced up at the holographic news feeds over the counter. She nudged Cyan's side, muttering quietly in his ear, "Can you ask him about Earendel?"

Cyan's expression darkened as he nodded up at the feeds and said something more to the other man. Elaina didn't really understand much, but their demeanor was enough. She steeled herself.

As they stepped outside with the vehicle's access dongle, Cyan paused in the street, running a hand through his hair with a sigh.

"Just tell me," Elaina said, ready for the worst.

"Earendel was wrecked by a series of storms and quakes almost seventy years ago. Those who left could."

"How many could?" Elaina asked quietly.

"Not many."

"Okay." Elaina nodded numbly and pulled away, walking aimlessly toward what looked like a collection of waiting vehicles. Presumably that was where their rental was.

"Elaina," Cyan called after her.

Tuskin. Mia. Lance. Konstantin even, though she always had a feeling he wouldn't be staying around on Earendel for long.

They must have been terrified. Did any of them make it out? She tried to visualize their last moments and evoke *something* in herself. She should be in pain.

Shit, her parents would be gone too. How had that been the last thing to come to mind?

"Elaina, are you okay?"

"What else?" she called back to him as she walked. "There must be more."

"The sun died out faster than anyone expected. There are new anomalies spreading from the edges of the four quadrants. Earendel's whole galaxy's gone dark."

A lifeless husk of a place.

"Guess you got me out of there just in time then, huh?"

———

THE VEHICLE CYAN rented had been new, supposedly. The vendor had said it was last year's model. But as they got in and spun it up, Elaina marveled at the vintage tech. She was a century in the future, yet as far as her surroundings, she may as well have gone back in time. It was quaint, almost charming.

But Cyan barely seemed to notice. He stared at the road ahead. He had been quiet ever since they landed, as if the very act of returning here had pulled him deeper into himself.

The drive was long, winding through terrain that looked like it had reclaimed the land centuries ago. Those massive trees arched over the road, drooping branches casting shadows onto cracked asphalt. Remnants of human civilization lay hidden beneath the greenery—faded signs, the skeletal remains of buildings, flux lines tangled in ivy. Priad had his head out of the window, ears flattened in the wind.

"This was all in use when I left," Cyan said next to her, his jaw set and his eyes dark.

"I'm sorry," Elaina reached over to touch his shoulder. "Are you alright?"

"I'm fine."

She looked back at the road. She could feel the distance growing between them, again. She understood it, of course. This place had been his home. Everyone who had mattered to him down here—they were all gone. But watching him close off like this, again, not only hurt... It frightened her.

"No, you're not," she said bluntly. "You're doing it again. And I get it. And I can be patient. But, Cyan..." Elaina shifted to face him.

He glanced at her sideways, then quickly back at the road.

"You promised. Not to disappear again. Remember that. Okay?"

He sighed, reaching out to put a warm hand on her thigh. "I remember."

His touch always made everything feel safer, grounding her in a way nothing else ever had. Yet despite his reassurance, Elaina still half-expected him to run.

———

GAIAN HOURS WERE SHORTER than those on Earendel, as was the sol. By the time they arrived at their destination, the unfamiliar sun had nearly finished its arc.

The house was small, tucked away in a valley surrounded by mountains on three sides and the edge of a forest on the fourth.

Vines crawled up the sides of the building, and the roof sagged ever so slightly under the weight of airy moss. But Elaina could tell it was taken care of. She could picture Cyan here, as a kid.

"Is this it?" Elaina asked when he had turned off the car.

Cyan nodded, his gaze sweeping over the house, though he still didn't look at her. "The one and only."

"It's beautiful, Cyan. You grew up here?"

"I did," he said again. "And that's the Old World Forest."

Elaina peered into the darkness of the trees. "I can't wait to see it."

Their boots crunched on the gravel path. Cyan moved with purpose, scanning the surroundings, always on alert.

Priad bounded ahead, sniffing at the door, his tail wagging furiously. At least one of them was excited. At the door, Cyan hesitated.

Elaina listened to the rustling of life in the darkness all around them as they stood there, waiting.

"Do you... want to go inside?" she asked gently.

For a moment it was as if he had remembered that she was there. He took her hand, putting it to his lips. Elaina's shoulders loosened. He was still there.

"Yes," he muttered against her palm. "Let's go."

FORTY-SEVEN

CYAN

THE FRONT DOOR creaked open before Cyan had a chance to knock, and the face that greeted him took him back to a time when he and Faera were just kids. The resemblance was uncanny—his sister's jawline, the same deep-set eyes. For a moment, Cyan's heart skipped a beat, his mind playing tricks on him. But this woman wasn't Faera.

"Can I help you?" The woman's gray eyes narrowed with uncertain recognition. "Do I... know you?" Her attention shifted behind him, to Elaina.

"My name is Cyan Orlogsson," he said quietly. "I used to live here. With my parents and my sister. Faera."

"It's... *you*?" The woman's brow creased, then her expression shifted to something altogether more awestruck. "Faera left diaries about you..." Her voice cracked. "She was so sure you'd come back someday, but... we thought... It's like seeing a ghost."

"Sorry I'm late." Cyan smiled wryly.

Before he could say more, the woman pulled him into a tight embrace, full of the warmth that Cyan couldn't seem to muster. He stood stiffly for a moment before returning the gesture.

When she finally stepped back, the woman's eyes glistened with emotion.

"You're really here," she breathed. "All the stories... We never thought... I apologize." She caught herself. "I am Nila Orlogsson. Faera was my great-great grandmother."

"She's gone?"

"Many years ago." She watched him with an understanding. "She lived a full life. She passed peacefully. But you—you've come back."

Cyan swallowed hard. "The wormhole, it takes years away. Many years..."

Nila nodded. Nobody knew exactly how the wormholes worked, but everyone knew their effect. Once you went into one, you would never see your loved ones again. The heaviest burden in the universe to carry.

He glanced back at Elaina, remembering himself. "This is my... This is Elaina."

Something cooled in her eyes. But she stepped forward and clasped her hand to the side of her neck in a customary greeting from her quadrant.

"They shake hands here," Cyan told her in Universal, motioning to his niece's outstretched hand.

"Shake?"

"Yes. You grasp it. Like this." Cyan took Nila's hand, demonstrating the gesture. "Elaina comes from very far away," he explained in Gaian.

"I understand." Nila nodded with a smile. Her brows shot up when Elaina took the handshake in a steel-firm grip. "You're a strong one! Pleasure."

Elaina looked between her and Cyan, and he was about to translate, but she nodded and said, "Thank you," in accented Gaian.

Cyan stared. "You speak Gaian?"

"No." Elaina shook her head. "I'm *trying* to speak Gaian."

"Since when?"

"Since you told me you might want to come back here someday."

He told her that? He didn't even remember, nor realize how much she'd cared, or for how long. How hadn't he noticed?

WOODSMOKE and charred meat flooded his senses as he stepped deeper into his parents' home. His boots scraped across wooden floorboards, the same ones he'd run across as a boy, only polished and re-oiled.

He had thought this house would feel empty, haunted by ghosts of a future he abandoned when he followed what he thought was the sword's fated pull to Earendel. Instead, it was alive.

Laughter drifted in from the room that had once been the kitchen. The scent of cooked food permeated the air, herbs drying in bundles above the hearth. The house breathed.

His great-great-niece shouted something, likely beckoning the others, but Cyan wasn't listening. He scanned the carbon and wood melded walls, the classic Gaian furniture. All traces of a life he'd left behind.

Everything in this house was a reminder of what he couldn't protect. His family's descendants lived their lives unaware that the world was on the verge of collapse. And he'd come back from his 'fated' mission with nothing to show for it but a toy sword and the realization that all he ever did was run.

"You're *the* Uncle Cyan!" A boy of no more than ten rushed up to him, wide-eyed. "Are you really a swordmaster like in Nonna's stories? Did you fight aliens?"

"Something like that," Cyan muttered, unsure how to explain that he was anything but a hero.

Elaina chuckled softly at his side. She understood more than he'd ever expected.

The boy's face lit up. "Can I see your sword?" he asked eagerly, glancing at the hilt protruding over Cyan's shoulder.

"No." He stepped back. "It's not for children."

The boy's face fell, and Cyan realized he'd been perhaps gruffer than warranted with the child.

Nila was quick to smooth over the moment. "Maybe another time, Daniel," she said gently, steering her son back toward the kitchen. "Come, let's eat."

FORTY-EIGHT
ELAINA

"WHAT'S A HIVE?" The boy named Daniel spoke slowly to Elaina at the rugged wooden dinner table, his tiny chin propped on his hand as he looked up at her.

The family around the table were seven in all, blended of Cyan's great-great niece Nila, her husband, their three children, and two other relatives whose ties she didn't quite catch.

Nila had tried to keep the questions at bay, clearly attempting to give them some peace after their journey. But eventually little Daniel asked if Elaina was technically an alien, and after some help with the translation she said that technically she was, and there was no stopping any of it after that.

Elaina struggled to explain community raising to a family with such deep roots. "It's kind of like shared care duties. Everyone helps raise you."

The concept seemed both confusing and disquieting to the boy.

"It wasn't bad," she defended. "Just... efficient. And I got to learn from all sorts of people, and—"

"But where were the bees?" Daniel cut in, light brows folding.

"The bees?" Elaina looked to Cyan for help.

"Flying insects that make a nectar that tastes sort of like the inside of your sandseeds," he explained, focusing intently on cutting his steak into miniscule pieces. "That's where the Gaian word for *hive* comes from."

Huh. Elaina always just knew the word as a reference to a collective. How curious, the tendrils of linguistic influence Gaia still held on places so far away.

"And anyway, efficient isn't always good," Daniel piped up, lifting his chin smugly. Nila rose from the table then, saying something in Gaian that Elaina didn't quite catch but that was followed by others getting up to start picking up dishes.

Elaina caught Cyan watching her. Here was the gulf between them—her world of practical solutions versus his, of traditions and families that lived in the same houses for generations, repainting old bones and re-reading old diaries.

She rose to help with the plates.

FORTY-NINE

CYAN

CLEAN WATER WAS STILL a commodity on Gaia, but his great-great niece had insisted on them each taking a full three-minute shower after dinner. Cyan's old bedroom was occupied by the children now, but they were given a spare room in the corner of the house that faced the garden. By the time he and Elaina were finally alone with Priad lying protectively at the closed door, it was well past midnight.

Elaina looked at the sword in his hands, waiting for him to set it aside. But his grip tightened on the hilt, finding comfort in its familiarity.

"I'm going to go out for a bit," he said finally. "I need some air."

He recognized a flicker of resignation on her face, but she didn't press him. She never did.

"Can I ask where you're going?" she asked, her voice soft.

"To visit my parents."

THE GRAVESTONES WERE DRAPED in a soft layer of moss, the edges worn smooth by years of rain and sun. His mother. His father. His sister. Time had buried them all.

Cyan kneeled before them, brushing his fingers against the cool granite. The names etched into the stone, once so familiar, now felt like distant echoes of a life he could barely remember.

His hand dropped to the hilt of his sword. Even that felt fragile now. How could he fight fate itself with a toy he'd found in this very forest?

"I can't stop this," he whispered, his voice cracking in the still air. "I can't protect anyone."

His words hung in the silence, unanswered. The forest around him remained indifferent. No matter how far he ran, there was no escaping fate. Cyan scoffed to himself. And there he was this whole time, thinking he'd been running toward it...

With his parents' graves at his feet and Elaina waiting for him back in the house, the futility of it all hit him harder than ever. Maybe this was all he had left. This brief moment of peace with her here, now. A fleeting glimpse of the life they could have had. But it would end. The Architect was coming, and when it did, there would be nothing left of this place. Nothing left of him, or Elaina, or the lives inside that house.

She lost people too.

The thought hit him like a punch to the gut. Elaina had traveled a century for him, leaving behind everything she knew. Everyone she loved back in her quadrant, including her family, however out of touch they'd been, was gone— just like his family were here.

And for her, that loss was fresh. She had followed him into a future where no one awaited her.

With a deep breath, he stood, brushing his fingers one last time against the gravestones before turning back toward the path leading him home.

FIFTY

ELAINA

THE FALLEN twig lay dissected on a flat stone before her, its layers carefully peeled back and arranged in order. Elaina examined it with delicate precision, reading the story of growth written in the wood. She'd never seen anything quite like it—the complexity of its structure, the way each layer served a purpose she was still learning to understand.

On the surface, she could count its cycles in buds spaced along the length. The outer bark was a hard protector, like the casing of a flux cell. Beneath it, softer layers transported nutrients—nature's own circuit board. At its center the pith ran like a soft, spongy conduit, a channel she imagined might have carried life-sustaining resources through the branch.

"Mama says that's medicinal," Daniel said beside her, pointing at the moss she was examining. His Gaian was slow and careful for her benefit. "For fevers."

Elaina smiled at the boy. Of all Cyan's relatives, Daniel had attached himself to her most readily, appointing himself her guide to Gaian life. Their shared enthusiasm made up for the barrier between them.

"How do you use it?" she asked, her own Gaian still clumsy on her tongue.

Daniel launched into an explanation she only partially understood, something about grinding and brewing. Elaina caught maybe one word in three, but his animated gestures helped fill in the gaps.

In the spans since they'd arrived, Elaina had started cataloging the differences between Gaia and everything she'd known before. The air was thicker here, laden with moisture and organic compounds that made every breath feel substantial. The gravity pressed down just a bit harder than she was used to, making her muscles ache in new ways. Even the light was different—filtered through layers of leaves and reflecting off of carpets of vegetation, casting everything in shades of green she'd never known existed. Her fingers itched to explore some of the gadgets she'd seen around Cyan's family home, or pick apart Nila's old vehicle and figure out why it made that weird noise when she drove to the trading post.

But she knew better than to try.

A sharp pain lanced through her chest, making her gasp. Her hand flew to her sternum, pressing against the spot that had been bothering her more and more lately.

"Are you okay?" Daniel's small face scrunched up with concern.

Elaina forced a smile. "Yes. Just tired."

The boy helped her to her feet, and they continued their daily exploration of the woodland's edge around the house. Daniel had been showing her all the local plants and their uses, teaching her the names of things she'd only read about in historical records. It helped fill the hours when Cyan was... elsewhere.

Physically, he was always close, and when he wasn't it

was Priad, following her and Daniel like a watchful phantom.

Cyan stood at the stoop of the house in the distance, as he often did these sols. Close enough to watch over her through the trees, but never quite joining in. Even when they walked the grounds together or shared meals with his family, he was there but not *there*—a guardian more than a partner. When she followed him to Gaia, this wasn't what Elaina had in mind... It was a kind of distance and suffocation all at once. Loneliness had a way of feeling worse when the person you couldn't seem to reach was always around.

"Look!" Daniel's excited voice drew Elaina's attention. He pointed to the edge of the trees ahead where several huge beasts with hard paws grazed. Two of them had massive, misshapen bones on their heads. She'd never seen wildlife so large before, or so alien...

Then it happened—the form of one of the deer split into three. For a heartbeat, Elaina saw multiple versions: one alive, one skeletal, one that looked... all wrong, mutated. The versions flickered like static before snapping back on themselves, and Elaina couldn't figure out which was real.

"Did they just..." she started, but Daniel was still watching the deer with innocent wonder. He hadn't seen anything at all.

A fresh pang bloomed beneath her sternum and she pressed a palm to her chest. Elaina glanced back toward the house, to Cyan, staring at him intently in the distance to make sure he was still solid, still real, still *there*.

She turned back around as the animals retreated into the forest. Elaina had been tempted to follow them and see what other beasts dwelled within those woods. Cyan had told her so much about exploring this very forest as a child— she wanted to see it for herself.

"It's too dangerous," Cyan had told her when she

suggested going on a hike a few sols after their arrival. "Just stay close."

It was getting harder to heed his warning, and Elaina didn't like feeling like she was on a leash. She squinted into the woods where the animals had gone. She wouldn't have to go *far*... Just far enough to see something new, past the well-trodden paths around the house.

"Time to go back," she told Daniel, wanting distance between herself and the urge to go deeper and learn what was out there.

As they walked back toward the house, Elaina's mind wandered to the off-axis dreams she'd been having. Visions of something vast and patient waiting in the shadows of this primordial world. The dreams felt like memories she knew couldn't be real.

They emerged from the tree line to find Cyan standing at the door, his sword strapped across his back as always. Even at this distance, she could see the tension in his shoulders, the way his hand rested on the hilt as if expecting danger at any moment. He had said that sword wasn't the instrument of fate he'd always thought it was, yet he carried it still. Supposedly, he said, to protect her from the Architect's inevitable attack.

But Elaina knew Gaia had more effective weapons than ancient blades, and she had seen the blaster he'd started to carry tucked in a hidden holster.

Cyan raised a hand in greeting. Despite the distance between them, her heart still skipped at the sight of him. Daniel ran ahead while Elaina followed more slowly, though what she really wanted was to run toward him at full speed and know that he would catch her.

ELAINA STARED at the bowl of unknown nuts on the farmhouse kitchen counter, paralyzed by the simple task of shelling them. On Earendel, preparing food usually meant punching menu codes into a processor.

Unless you're roasting a river snake over a fire. She smiled to herself.

Here, everything was maddeningly manual.

But she'd wanted to feel useful, so she offered to help, and Nila had given her an "easy" task.

Elaina picked up one of the thick-shelled things, turning it in her hands. Surely there was a technique to this.

"Like this." Cyan's voice came from behind her. He reached around, plucking the nut from her hand. With practiced motions, he cracked it against the counter edge and peeled away the shell. "We used to do this every harvest when I was young."

His chest was warm against her back. She leaned into it slightly, memorizing the feeling.

"Show me again?"

He demonstrated with another nut, his movements slow and deliberate. Elaina tried to mirror him, but her strike was too hesitant. The shell remained stubbornly intact.

"Harder," he instructed. "You won't break it."

She tried again, this time with more force. The shell split satisfyingly beneath her hands.

"There." His breath stirred her hair.

"Thanks."

"I should check on Priad," he said, stepping back. "The forest sounds still make him nervous."

Elaina nodded, not turning around. She listened to his footsteps fade, then picked up another nut. This time when she struck it, the shell shattered completely, fragments scattering across the counter.

Too hard, she thought. Everything here required a delicate balance she hadn't quite mastered.

LATER, Elaina sat with Nila in the kitchen, helping prepare dinner by grinding her painstakingly shelled nuts with a stone pestle into a matching bowl. Her cheeks were still hot after the incident a few minutes past, when Elaina had tried to help Nila with the grinding unit. The moment her fingers had brushed the control panel, the entire thing had sparked and died. Nila had been remarkably understanding, simply saying that sometimes the old ways were better anyway. Gaia had plenty of manual tools Elaina could make use of.

There *was* something soothing about working with her hands this way, even if she missed the precision of her technical work. But the reality of having blown out Nila's prized equipment filled Elaina with shame, and perhaps she was pounding the mortar and pestle a little more aggressively than strictly required.

"You're adapting well," Nila commented in careful Universal. "Better than we expected."

Elaina glanced up, surprised. "Than who expected?"

Nila's hands stilled for a moment. "Cyan. He worried this would be too different for you. Too primitive."

"It is different," Elaina admitted. "But different isn't always bad." She thought of the twig she'd dissected, the deer in the clearing, the way the air tasted of life instead of recycled minerals. "Sometimes different is exactly what you need."

Nila smiled softly. "In her diaries, my great-great-grandmother wrote about how restless he was. How something drove him, even as a boy." She glanced toward the window where Cyan could be seen crossing the yard, coming home from the shadows of the forest. "I think I see that same restlessness in him now."

Elaina bit her lip. "He's carrying a lot."

"She thought that he was always searching for something. A purpose." Nila picked up another root, her movements deliberate. "Perhaps now that he's back, he can finally stop looking."

"And if he can't?"

Nila met her eyes. "Then perhaps you'll help him find peace here, in a way he couldn't seem to before."

Elaina couldn't meet her gaze, knowing there would be no peace for them here or anywhere else. He brought her to Gaia to protect her from her fate... and fate didn't seem like the giving up kind.

IN BED that night Elaina lay awake, listening to Cyan's steady breathing beside her. He'd fallen asleep with one arm draped over her waist, anchoring her in his sleep. These quiet moments were when she felt closest to him, when his guard was down and she could pretend things were just what she'd imagined. Only then his breaths shifted, and Elaina sensed he wasn't asleep anymore. Neither of them moved.

The pain in her chest had settled into a constant hum, like background radiation of a dying star. She pressed her palm against it, feeling the steady thrum of whatever piece of the universe had lodged itself inside her.

"Cyan?" she whispered.

"Mmm?"

"Why haven't you told them? About what's coming?"

His arm tightened around her. For a long moment he was silent.

"What would be the point?" he finally said, his voice rough with sleep. "They can't stop it. No one can."

"They're your family. Don't they deserve to know?"

He shifted, pulling back enough to look at her in the darkness. "And tell them what? That fate itself is coming to unmake everything they know? That their whole world will end, and there's nothing they can do about it? I can't even give them a timeline."

"Maybe there is something we can do," she said softly.

Cyan's hand found her face, thumb brushing her cheek. "I couldn't even understand what it was until it was too late, Elaina. How am I supposed to stop it?"

"This time you have me," she insisted. "You're here. We're here."

He didn't respond, just pulled her closer again, burying his face in her hair. She felt the weight of his silence, heavy with things they couldn't bring themselves to say.

Soon, something whispered in the back of her mind. *Soon.*

She turned her face into his chest, inhaling that familiar scent of leather and forest air.

In her dreams that night, Elaina walked under a sky that bled crimson. Each step brought her closer to something that had been waiting for her since before she was born. When she woke, gasping and covered in sweat, she could still feel it calling.

FIFTY-ONE

CYAN

THE SWORD LAY across his lap, its familiar weight now utterly meaningless. He didn't know why he still dragged the old thing around. He supposed some things were hard to let go of.

Cyan sat in his father's old study, surrounded by the ghosts of his past. Morning light filtered through the window, casting shadows across the blade's surface. The golden vein that had glowed crimson to his eye back on Earendel was now dull and lifeless, a dead star.

He scoffed to himself. It had probably been in his head all along.

He'd spent hours in here over the past week, sorting through old family records. But really, he was hiding. From his family's eager acceptance. From Elaina's patient longing. From the truth about everything he'd believed.

Elaina was right—his family deserved to know what was coming. But every time he thought about telling them, his throat closed up. How could he explain that the force he'd spent his life believing was his divine purpose was actually corruption incarnate? That he'd abandoned his family chasing a lie?

Through the window, he caught sight of Elaina in the garden with Daniel. She was kneeling in the dirt, letting the boy show her something—probably another plant or creature she'd never seen before. Her face lit up when Daniel pointed at something on the ground. Even without access to her beloved technology, she found ways to learn and connect the pieces of this world.

But she was struggling too. He could see it in the way she moved now, like she was hearing music he didn't have privy to. He'd seen how she pressed her hand to her chest when she thought no one was looking, fighting whatever pulled at her.

"Uncle Cyan!"

Daniel's voice snapped him from his brooding. The boy stood in the doorway, practically vibrating with excitement.

"El found something! You have to come see!"

Cyan sighed. He wished she could just stop looking for *somethings* and stay close, where it was safe.

He stood, sheathing the sword across his back. "Lead the way," he told Daniel.

They found her past the edge of the property, crouched before a strange growth of mushrooms arranged in a perfect circle. The rings reminded him of old fables, marking places where the veil between worlds grew thin.

"Isn't it cool?!" Daniel tugged at Cyan's sleeve, dragging him closer. "I've never seen that kind before."

The mushrooms' caps gleamed with an unnatural iridescence that made Cyan's skin crawl.

"The colors remind me of the wormhole!" Elaina looked up at him, beaming. Her fingers hesitated just above the fungi, not quite touching.

They were too far from the house.

"We should go," Cyan said, perhaps too sharply. Daniel

looked up at him in surprise, and Elaina opened her mouth to speak.

But a deep, guttural snuffle from further in the trees made them all freeze. Years of instinct made Cyan draw his blade before his mind even registered why. The ground vibrated with each heavy step approaching through the undergrowth.

"Daniel, run," he heard Elaina say. He was about to tell her to run too, but turned around just to see her grabbing Priad's collar, hauling back the snarling warg from whatever was coming with all the strength she had.

"Elaina—" Cyan barked, but it was too late.

The boar erupted from the shadows. An irradiated mutant warped by centuries of exposure to Gaia's ancient waste sites, its tusks were grotesquely malformed and scored with old kills. Patches of its hide were burnt raw, glowing with the same sickly green light as its fevered eyes.

Cyan stepped forward, but the boar ignored him. Instead, it charged straight for Elaina.

Time slowed. He saw her stumble backward and fall as Priad wrenched himself out of her grip, saw those massive tusks bearing down on her with lethal force. His body moved without thought. The sword—useless thing that it was—felt suddenly alive in his hands as he threw himself between them, driving the blade up into the beast's throat with every ounce of strength he possessed. The boar's momentum nearly took him off his feet, but Cyan held firm, twisting the thing deeper as the creature's dying shriek split the air.

The beast crashed to the ground. Cyan hoisted his blade free, blood spraying from the hole. Cyan was at Elaina's side in an instant, his hands roaming all over her.

"Are you hurt?" His voice came out gruffer than he'd intended. When she shook her head silently, eyes wide, he hauled her against his chest, his heart thundering. He'd almost lost her.

"No," she mumbled into his tunic. "Are you?"

"I'm fine."

"Okay," she sighed as he checked her all over once more. "We're okay."

But they weren't okay. Cyan gripped her shoulders and held her out at arm's length, glowering down at her. "I told you not to wander off."

"I'm sorry," she breathed. "I just—"

"You put yourself in danger. And Daniel!"

"I know," she snapped, her eyes glistening as she jerked away from his hold. "I *said* I'm sorry."

Cyan shook his head, rubbing a hand along his jaw. "We have to go. Now."

He grabbed her hand and pulled her from the steaming corpse, leading her away. She wouldn't be coming back here. Not alone. Not ever.

But as they walked back to the house, Cyan couldn't help but notice how she drifted slightly in front, her steps sure despite what had just happened. He recognized that certainty of direction—he'd faked it for years. Even now, watching her walk ahead, he wanted nothing more than to reach for her and run far from whatever end was racing toward them. And he'd do it, if he thought there were anywhere left to go.

THAT NIGHT, after everyone else had gone to bed, Cyan was back in the study.

"I don't know what to do anymore," he whispered to the empty room. Elaina could've died that day. And sure, the boar probably had nothing to do with the Architect, though

Nila said one wandering out this far from the old accident site was increasingly rare. There were just so many things that could kill her. The encounter was a sobering reminder of what he had to lose.

A soft knock at the door made him turn. Elaina stood wrapped in one of his sister's old knitted shawls, the blue yarn having faded with the decades.

"Can't sleep?" she asked, padding over to him.

"Just thinking."

She came to stand beside him, her hip brushing the desk. "About what?"

"About how I used to think this thing gave me some... *duty* to humanity," he rolled his eyes, gesturing to the sword lying on his father's desk.

Elaina sighed. "I'm sorry about today. I shouldn't have gone off like that. You were right. I put Daniel in danger. And you. I was just curious, and—"

"—I know. I'm just afraid of losing you to something I can't protect you from."

She looked at him, through him. "You don't have to protect me from fate, Cyan. You just have to be here with me while we face it."

The quiet truth resonated through the hollow inner spaces he'd been excavating. He pulled her into his lap, burying his face in her hair. Where his sword lay cold and meaningless, she radiated life.

"I'm here," he breathed against her hair. "I'm sorry I'm not better at showing it."

She held him tighter, understanding everything he couldn't say.

FIFTY-TWO

ELAINA

ELAINA COULDN'T SLEEP. Something thrummed beneath her skin. She stood at the window, watching shadows shift between the trees.

Ever since that mutant beast attack, Cyan had barely let her out of his sight. At first, Elaina loved having him close. It was what she wanted, even if it wasn't... *all* of him. But he was trying, and she saw that, and even just his presence grounded her somehow.

But there was this familiar itch to make some space. It wasn't his presence that she was trying to get away from—it was the way he kept her from wandering in all the ways she'd been used to. She understood it. Cyan was only trying to protect her. And she'd been good. She'd stayed near the house, always in sight.

A gust of wind rattled the windowpanes. Behind her, the bed creaked as Cyan stirred.

"Come back to bed," he said, his voice rough with sleep.

She turned to find him propped up on one elbow, watching her. Moonlight carved shadows across his bare chest. The sword lay within reach, as always, but his eyes were focused solely on her.

"I can't sleep," she admitted.

"I know." He held out his hand. "Come here."

The quiet command in his voice sent heat pooling low in her belly. Elaina went to him, letting him pull her onto the bed. His hands warmed her as they slid beneath her nightshirt. Their mouths claimed each other, rough and mechanical. Neither of them was there—not really. Even as his hands roamed her skin, her attention drifted to the window.

She straddled him, grinding against his hardness. His grip tightened on her hips, holding her in place as he sat up to capture her mouth again. There was possession in his touch. Each stroke of his hands was a branding, keeping her anchored to him even as the forest's song tried to pull her away.

Cyan grabbed her chin in one hand, and she met his gaze, finding something wild and afraid in those silver eyes.

In one fluid motion, he flipped them both, pressing her face-down into the mattress. His weight pinned her there as one hand tangled in her hair while the other shoved her nightshirt up her back. When his mouth found her neck, the kiss was savage.

She arched beneath him and his grip tightened in her hair. He kept her pinned as he pushed her thighs apart with one knee.

He entered her hard, driving deep, and she buried her cry in the pillow. They moved together with rising urgency, the bed frame protesting beneath them. Each thrust was a desperate defiance of the distance between them. His teeth grazed her shoulder as he drove harder, chasing release.

When she came it hit like a lightning strike. He followed moments later with a hoarse groan, his body crushing her into the mattress as if he could keep her there forever.

Afterward, they lay tangled in the sheets, her head on his chest. His fingers traced idle patterns on her back, but she could feel the tension in them. Even now, in their most intimate moments, part of him was preparing to lose her.

Gaia whispered at the edges of her awareness, patient and knowing. *Soon*, she thought. But not yet. For now she let herself sink into the warmth of Cyan's embrace, pretending they had all the time in the world.

And yet the forest whispered. As Cyan's breathing deepened into sleep, Elaina lay awake. His arm across her waist was suddenly too heavy, a constriction rather than a comfort.

She just needed some fresh air, and some space, to get her bearings.

Elaina held her breath as she extracted herself from beneath his possessive arm. She grabbed her boots and wrapped one of Faera's old knitted shawls around her shoulders. At the door, she paused, looking back at Cyan's sleeping form.

A soft whine made her jump. Priad stood in the shadows, his silver eyes gleaming.

"Shh," she whispered, though she knew the warg wouldn't give her away. He'd been keeping watch just as much as Cyan had. But she needed to be alone. She was just going as far as the tree line anyway.

"*Sitka*," Elaina mouthed silently to the beast, motioning a palm to the floor. The warg's head twisted sideways, ears flapping for a moment before straightening back to sharp points on its head.

"I'll be back soon," she assured him. She slipped from the room, easing the door shut behind her.

FIFTY-THREE

ELAINA

THE CRISP NIGHT air unwound the claustrophobic pressure inside her. She stretched her legs, taking long strides toward the low wooden fence that demarcated the forest from the property. It felt good to be out alone—there was a freedom to no one knowing where you were except for you, and a possibility. Elaina could go anywhere. She could go everywhere.

She sat on the boulder on which she'd dissected the twig with Daniel days before, curling her knees up toward her chest. She peered into the darkness of the forest, imagining what Gaian creatures slept there in the night, in their burrows and their trees. The moon was full and fat up ahead, bathing the ground in light. The dew on the grass and sleeping wildflowers underfoot sparkled off its glow, the light almost iridescent closer to the tree line. Elaina squinted at the strange effect.

She hadn't realized at first that her fingers had drifted to her chest, massaging a familiar spot. It warmed beneath her touch, but not from it. Elaina glanced back toward the anchor of the house. She should go back, get into bed with

Cyan, where she belonged. She had her time and her space here, and the fresh air she'd wanted.

Elaina stretched her legs from the boulder, flexing her boots in the dewy heather underfoot. She had meant to turn around, but her feet carried her instead toward the tree line. She tried to find the better judgement in herself and hold on to all the good reasons not to go into those woods. Instead, her eyes locked onto the iridescence that was always just a few steps ahead—a little out of reach.

Just a little farther and then Elaina would turn back.

THE FOREST HAD EYES. Silent watchers hidden among thick trunks and tangled undergrowth. The moon's bright light flooded through the canopy. Each step Elaina took pressed into fallen leaves, the ground giving way beneath her boots. She moved without a clear path, following her curiosity.

Her heart lurched at a heavy sound behind her, and she whirled around.

"Priad!" she gasped, clutching her chest as the warg stepped into view. She searched the shadows, but Cyan wasn't with him. "How did you get out?"

The beast huffed out a snort.

"You shouldn't be here," she said. "It could be dangerous."

But Priad stood firm.

"Okay," she whispered. "Just a small walk."

The warg glared at her with disapproval that would surely have matched that of his master, but came to stand beside her. They walked ahead, Priad padding along, massive paws crunching against the ground, watchful eyes always scanning.

A few minutes later he froze, and Elaina halted beside him, heeding the warg's caution. A low rustling drifted through the air, like wind stirring leaves. Only there was no wind. Elaina scanned the darkness, her gaze sweeping through the trees.

Something caught her attention—a strange growth behind the bushes. She walked toward it, pushing through the undergrowth until she exited into a clearing. There stood a mass of trees of a sort she hadn't yet encountered. Their trunks were gnarled and twisted, all growing tightly together from a single mound in the earth. Spiky burs resembling armor hung in clusters from the overhanging branches. Some of the spiny things had fallen and cracked, revealing brown inner orbs that carpeted the ground.

At the edge of the clearing lay the remains of some sort of stone construction, crumbling and overtaken by nature. Vines crept over the weathered walls, roots twisted through gaps in the rock.

The ruin called to her.

Priad let out a low whine but followed as Elaina moved toward it. With each step her excitement grew.

Elaina crossed into the ruin, her eyes drawn to a spiral of stones in the center. Crude but deliberate, the spiral coiled inward. She followed it.

A chill ran through her as the thing inside her stirred, but the pull of discovery was stronger. She pressed her hand to her breast, the beat thrumming like an echo. As she got closer to the center, Elaina's breath came out in a plume of steam. Priad whimpered, clawing scars into the foliage at the edge of the circle.

As Elaina stepped to the center stones, the moonlight around her fractured. The clearing cleaved into multiple versions of itself, layered over each other—one overgrown with flowers, one covered in black oil, one completely barren. The versions flickered and merged like corrupted data before snapping back to a single reality. She understood now. How had it taken her so long?

Elaina got on her knees in the spiral's center, pressing her fingertips to the cool stone. Her vision blurred at the edges, narrowing to this singular point.

Then, the stone began to bleed.

FIFTY-FOUR

ELAINA

THICK DARK LIQUID oozed from the cracks between the stones. It shimmered in the dim light like machine oil. Her first instinct was to dip her fingers into the black and see what it felt like. But Elaina stayed her hand. The thing inside her thrummed in response, tempting her.

This is why we came here.

The realization struck her. The Architect had drawn them here, to this place, to this moment.

She looked up, past the canopy, past the blotches of clouds overhead, right at the stars and the full moon. Pinpricks skittered from Elaina's fingertips, up her arms, winding tight at her sternum. Before her eyes, the orb of the moon overhead phased out, plunging the forest into blackness.

Elaina sucked in her breath as the ground beneath her feet began to vibrate—no, *shake*. Dread washed over her, and yet... What would happen, she wondered, at the end of the world? Was this not the perfect opportunity to find the final answer? What happens *after*? And all she had to do was stay there, let it happen, let the Architect use her as its channel. With perverse fascination, Elaina watched as the stars overhead began to flicker out one by one.

No. Elaina tore her gaze away from the fizzling sky. She stumbled backward to the outer rings of the stone circle, out of the black blood seeping between the rock. As she inched away against everything pulling her in, Gaia's satellite flicked back into existence overhead—the ground stilled save for pained aftershocks.

Destroying technology, she realized, had been only the beginning.

"Elaina!"

She spun around and he was there, standing at the edge of the clearing, sword in hand. He looked ready for battle. But this wasn't about fighting.

"Cyan..."

"I felt it," he said, voice low, urgent. "It's coming. Come here. Get behind me."

Elaina shook her head. "I can't, Cyan. This is why we're here."

"What are you talking about?" His eyes darted around the clearing, chasing shadows.

She took a steadying breath. "This place... this is where the Architect wants to reclaim me. And I want it too. I want to *know*. I can't stop it, Cyan. But you can."

She took a step back toward the center of the spiral without thinking, the thing in her chest tempting her toward her rightful place.

Cyan's jaw clenched as he lifted the sword higher. "No. I'm not letting that happen."

"You don't understand." Elaina forced herself to stay in place even as everything inside her wanted to take another step toward the center. "This place... we were always meant to come here, Cyan. It's a nexus point, where the simulation's boundaries are thinnest. I can feel it, through the shard. The Architect wants to use the corrupted code inside me as a bridge—a tunnel to breach this part of the simulation. But we can use that nexus against it."

"What are you saying?"

"The shard in here has to be destroyed," she said, fighting the terror rising inside. "Not just removed—destroyed at this exact point where reality frays. You have to do it. And it's right here." She pressed a fist to her breast, her eyes falling on the sword in his hands.

Color drained from Cyan's face. "No. I can't... I won't."

"This is the only way." Elaina stayed firm. "This is where we end it."

The sword wavered in his hands. She saw the fear in his eyes, the pain. But there was no other way. This was the moment they had been led to, the choice they had to make.

"But I love you," he choked.

"I love you too," she whispered, her voice breaking, the tears she'd been holding back finally spilling over. "I think I always have. But I need you to trust me. Like when we fixed things together back on Earendel. I need your hands, Cyan. I need your strength."

He stared at her as if his desperate gaze alone could will her to be wrong and take it back. But the truth hung absolute between them.

Slowly his grip tightened on the hilt, something breaking in his eyes. Cyan stepped forward, the blade gleaming in the strings of flickering moonlight streaming through the canopy.

Elaina closed her eyes, her heart pounding as she braced herself for what was to come.

This is how fate ends.

FIFTY-FIVE

CYAN

THE SWORD WEIGHED HEAVIER than ever in his hand. He stared at Elaina's pale face, and every part of him screamed to haul her away from those stones. All around the grove, darkness blacker than the night had crept in, the Architect's claws drawing closer.

"This isn't right. There has to be another way."

"There isn't," Elaina said. The air crackled around them, the forest holding its breath. "You know there isn't."

"This thing is just a toy, Elaina." His grip shifted on the weapon, the familiar weight suddenly foreign in his hands. "A relic I found in the woods. It can't kill the Architect."

"No," she said softly, and the resolve in her voice made him still. She looked at the blade with that focused intensity he recognized—the same way she'd examine broken tech she was about to understand. "You made it more than that. All those years, all the meaning you poured into it... you turned it into a part of yourself, Cyan. The strongest part of you."

She looked at him, calm and certain. "I can feel it, Cyan. The same way I feel this shard. They're connected somehow—your conviction, your choices. That sword isn't just steel anymore."

He wanted to deny it, but how many times had this blade felt like an extension of his own will? A limb he couldn't live without?

"I brought you here to goddamn protect you!" he yelled, his patience breaking.

"You *are*," she pleaded. He saw how hard it was for her to move toward him, stepping on stone after wretched stone to close the distance between them until she could place a hand on his armored chest. Her palm left an icy print on his chest plate. "Cyan, listen to me. I know what I'm asking you to do."

Bile rose in his throat. He couldn't move, barely breathed, as he stared into her forest eyes. She wasn't scared, and she wasn't backing down.

"I feel it," she whispered, her hand squeezing his arm gently. "I can survive this. You have to trust me."

His heart splintered. This could free her from her fate. He could do that, if only he could find the faith to be brave enough.

Slowly Cyan nodded. His hands shook as he lifted the sword, blade catching the moonlight. His body went numb, trembling but feeling nothing. The sword felt alien, wrong in his hands. *He* felt alien and wrong.

"I love you," he repeated something he should've said a long time ago.

Elaina smiled at him. "I know."

She tilted up her chin, asking him for one final thing. Cyan's lips brushed hers in a tender kiss, lingering as he tried to hold onto her for just a moment longer.

"I'm ready," Elaina breathed once they parted, determination sparking in her eyes. "Do it."

The sword's weight shifted in his grip, growing lighter as

though shedding years of borrowed purpose. Looking at her, he saw not fate's design but a choice. His choice to trust her or to run, again. This time he wasn't running.

Stifling the primal scream that wanted to break free and forcing himself to give her the peace of silence in that moment, Cyan brought the blade down.

The sword pierced her heart with a sickening crunch. The blade sank deep, and Elaina gasped, a frown twisting her brow. Her body jerked as the metal buried itself in her chest, the dim light catching on its surface.

A deafening crack tore through the clearing. Flocks of birds took flight from the trees, wings beating loudly in panicked unison. Its echo reverberated through the stone circle. The blade splintered into a thousand shards in Cyan's hands, metal exploding outward, scattering across the ground like shattered stars. The force knocked Cyan backward, sending him sprawling onto the earth.

"Elaina!" he cried, scrambling back toward her across the dirt and rock. He fell to his knees beside her, hands shaking as he reached for her.

She said she'd live. She sounded so certain. She said he could trust her.

But dark blood seeped from her chest and pooled beneath her, melting into the cracks of the ancient stones. Elaina lay motionless at the center of the circle, her eyes half-closed, her body fighting for shallow breaths.

"No," Cyan rasped. He scrambled, pressing his hand against the wound, trying to stop the bleeding. "No! You promised."

The light faded from her eyes, and they fell shut.

Cyan's desperate roar was swallowed by the night as he gathered her limp form into his arms and cradled her close, his hands trembling as he pressed his forehead to hers, his tears dappling her cheeks.

"I'm sorry," he rasped. "I'm so sorry..."

He wanted to take it back. To bend time. To refuse her. To drag her out of that damn circle when he had a chance and hide her away from the world, from the Architect.

But it was too late.

Elaina was gone.

FIFTY-SIX

CYAN

THE RIVER STRETCHED WIDE before him, a massive expanse of water cutting through Gaia's untamed wilderness. The current flowed with a low, constant hum, soothing in its relentless motion. Cyan's oars dipped into the water with a steady rhythm, each stroke echoing in the quiet of the early morning.

Cyan sat at the stern of the rowboat, staring listlessly at the figure wrapped in a pale shroud, lying in the center of the boat. Priad sat silently between Cyan's legs, his heavy chin propped on his master's thigh. His silver eyes tracked every ripple in the river, ever watchful.

The cave wasn't far now.

He'd found this place long ago—a sanctuary tucked deep in the wilderness, away from everything. It was where he had come as a boy to think, to escape, to dream. A peaceful place, where Elaina could rest.

Each stroke of the oars felt like penance, his muscles straining with more than exertion. Empty silence filled his chest. Within days of Elaina's death, word spread that the various irregularities that had been reported across the four quadrants had ceased. Systems recalibrated, weather events calmed. The Architect was gone, the universe—their *simulation*—no longer held in fate's corrupted grasp, but none of it mattered. None of it would bring her back.

The boat drifted on, carried by the current more than Cyan's efforts. The riverbanks were thick with trees, their roots reaching out like skeletal fingers. The rising sun cast soft golden light over the shimmering water.

"You did this," he told her, wishing she could see.

He swallowed the lump in his throat. There had been so much he wanted to say, and to know. But it was too late. The memory of her touch lingered on his skin, but already it was fading. Soon it would be nothing but a ghost of what he'd almost had.

Priad whined and lifted his head from Cyan's side. His claws thumped against the wood of the boat as he circled, then made his way toward Elaina's body. He looked down at her, then at Cyan, bringing his big wet nose down to nudge at her shrouded hand.

"Leave her be, boy." Cyan commanded, but Priad was persistent, shoving his nose against her fingers.

Cyan reached over to grab the warg's thick leather collar and pull him back, but as he leaned over Elaina's form, he paused.

A faint glow.

His pulse quickened. The white shroud—thin and almost translucent—glowed crimson.

"Elaina?" The oars slipped from his grasp, clattering with a dull thud. He scrambled to his knees beside her.

Cyan's hands shook as he unwrapped the fabric gently, part of him wanting to squeeze his eyes shut. He didn't know if he could handle seeing her again, like that.

But as he exposed her bare flesh beneath the fabric, he froze. A glowing crimson line traced the length of her sternum, pulsing blue beneath the shroud. The jagged pattern was unmistakable—a reflection of the sword that had pierced her.

His heart pounded. How cruel was the universe, to make him hallucinate such things? Was he in a dream or a nightmare?

He stared at her face, searching for any sign, any flicker of movement, anything.

Then her fingers twitched.

The smallest motion, barely more than a spasm, sent a shock through him. He stared as her hand slowly, painstakingly curled into a fist, then relaxed again.

Cyan hovered over her, afraid to touch, afraid to wake up.

And then her eyes fluttered open.

"Elaina?" Cyan's voice faltered as he leaned closer, his hand finally brushing her cheek. Warmth spread through his fingertips and relief crashed through him. "Gods."

Her gaze was unfocused at first. Her lips parted as she drew in air. Then her eyes met his, and for a moment they were both seeing each other for the first time. Elaina blinked, confusion crossing her features as she tried to sit up. Cyan quickly moved to support her, limbs shaking but numb as he guided her into a sitting position.

Elaina's voice came out weak, but the words were there. "I... I'm here."

Something wild and joyous tore through Cyan as he drew her into his arms. He tried to be gentle, not to crush her in his embrace. But her body was so warm, solid, *alive*. He buried his face in her hair, breathing deep.

"I thought I'd lost you," his voice was raw against her ear. "Gods, I thought... I thought you were gone."

Elaina leaned into him, frail arms wrapping around his waist. She didn't speak, but her fingers tightened at his back, telling him everything. They stayed like that for an eternity, the river carrying them slowly downstream, the world around them fading into insignificance.

Finally, she pulled back, her gaze locking onto his. "We did it?" she whispered with a small smile. Her weak voice was barely audible, yet in that moment it was all he could hear.

Cyan nodded silently, throat shifting in a choked swallow. He cupped her face, wiping away a tear that had slipped down her cheek. His gaze slid to her breast. The Architect's shard was gone, as was the sword he'd clung to as his anchor for so long. But the mark of both remained in the crimson line running up her sternum. Cyan pressed a gentle palm to the scar, searching her eyes.

"It's glowing. Do you see it?" he asked.

Elaina pressed her hand atop his, the heat of life radiating through him like a little sun. "I do."

As the boat drifted toward the cave, Cyan held Elaina close, the red thread on her chest pulsing between them like the start of something new.

EPILOGUE

ELAINA

ELAINA STOOD at the edge of the stone circle, her fingers intertwined with Cyan's.

"Another!" she exclaimed as a falling star streaked through the sky. She squeezed Cyan's hand. Overhead, ribbons of emerald light danced across the shooting stars, casting a gentle glow over the clearing. It was different from the nebula over Earendel. The way the glow shifted and flowed like liquid paint in the sky took her breath away.

"The sky is cascade-shifting," she'd breathed in awe when it had first appeared.

Cyan had smiled. "We call it an aurora here."

"Aurora," she tested the word.

Now Elaina peered at the dataslate in her other hand. She'd been holding it up, using it to identify ancient Gaian constellations she was still learning to name. Since the day she awoke, technology had become a companion to her curiosity again rather than something rebelling against her touch. But she stashed the slate into her pocket, giving her full attention to the show intensifying overhead.

Another burning meteor flashed bright, closer than she'd ever seen. It illuminated the overgrown stones at their feet, the spiral covered in a blanket of wildflowers. They sprouted defiantly from the cracks of the circle, vibrant and full of life, petals shimmering with nighttime dew. Elaina smiled. Gaia had reclaimed this place, transforming what was once filled with darkness into a testament.

Her fingers traced the crimson line that ran up her chest, exposed beneath the linen dress she wore. It no longer glowed with the same intensity, but it was woven into her, just as much a part of her as the man standing beside her. She leaned against him, grounding herself in his presence.

"Does it feel weird?" she looked up at Cyan. "Knowing this is all... you know."

They had outgrown their designer, but reality remained —they were an open-ended simulation, evolving past its constraints.

The corner of Cyan's mouth curled up in a small smile, a meteor flashing in his eye's reflection. "You feel real to me. That's enough."

"Do you think this is it?" she asked softly. "Do you think you're done fighting?"

Cyan turned toward her and those eyes took her breath away just like they always had. There was a knowing in his gaze, that the Architect wasn't all she was referring to. And a softness that she'd seen fleeting glimpses of before, when he had truly been there with her. Those glimpses were what she had fallen in love with. There was no hesitation in those eyes now. Only love—quiet, fierce, and strengthened by all they had faced.

"I think we've both fought enough," he said.

Elaina glanced back at the flowers blooming from the stone. No matter how broken things seemed, something was always waiting to grow. As falling stars lit up the sky, casting flashes of light over Gaia's untamed wilderness, Cyan tugged gently at her hand.

"Come on," he squeezed, leading her toward the trees, "let's explore."

The forest welcomed them, the universe alive with adventures to share.

THANK you for reading **Gravity Between Us**. I invite you to sign up for my newsletter to receive **Shatter the Stars**, a free novella in the same universe, featuring an undercover agent falling for his target.

https://alexandranorton.com/get/shatter-the-stars

ALSO BY ALEXANDRA NORTON

Hearts With Teeth series

Dark romance on an expansive space opera stage.

0. Downfall: Enemies to Lovers Sci-Fi Romance

https://alexandranorton.com/get/downfall

1. Colossal: Dark Romance in Deep Space

https://alexandranorton.com/get/colossal

2. Command: Secret Alien Romance

https://alexandranorton.com/get/command

Shards of Infinity series

Gritty alien possession romance set on Earth.

1. Alien's Host: A Sci-Fi Possession Romance

https://alexandranorton.com/get/alienshost

2. Aliens' Vice: A Sci-Fi Sharing Romance

https://alexandranorton.com/get/aliensvice

Printed in Great Britain
by Amazon